D0196473

OUR SECRET LIFE IN THE MOVIES

OUR
SECRET
LIFE
IN THE
MOVIES

By Michael McGriff
& J. M. Tyree

A
STRANGE
OBJECT
Austin, Texas

Published by
A Strange Object
astrangeobject.com

ISBN 978-0-9892759-6-5

Cover illustration and design by M. S. Corley
Book design by Amber Morena

CONTENTS

ABOUT *OUR SECRET LIFE IN THE MOVIES*

We wrote *Our Secret Life in the Movies* in San Francisco, in a shared sublet a block away from Mission Dolores, the site of Carlotta Valdes's grave in Hitchcock's *Vertigo*. We'd hatched a plan to watch every film in the Criterion Collection's sweeping catalog of world cinema classics over the course of a single year. This obsession fed off pizza boxes, sambuca fumes, and whatever is damaged on the Y chromosome.

We watched film after film—as many as two or three a day—and wrote stories inspired by them. For each film, two stories, a double take. After completing a dozen sketches, it became obvious that we were writing a fragmented book of linked snapshots chronicling our parallel trajectories as the last children of the Cold War, coming of age in the 1980s amidst the white noise of intercontinental-ballistic mayhem and Reaganomics.

We all have a secret life in the movies, in which the pictures seep through our dreams until fantasy and reality become hopelessly blurred. We are in the movies, and the movies are in us.

MM / JMT
2014

OUR SECRET LIFE IN THE MOVIES

PORQUE TE VAS

\ After *Cría Cuervos* by Carlos Saura \

In 1973, my local fame as a defective birth—holes in both lungs—spread to a Rosicrucian prayer group in Milwaukee. They chanted some incantations that mended the fabric of the universe for a time. For example, that same month, the final combat soldiers left Vietnam and Captain Beefheart declared that whales had high IQs "from what I hear of their music." My lungs healed while Nixon's White House crumbled. The Pioneer 11 spacecraft hurtled toward Jupiter and Saturn, eventually collecting an Emmy for its photographs of the outer planets and becoming the first human object to leave the solar system. Humanity lost contact with Pioneer 11 in 1995, the same year I left

1

town, but fortunately both of us are attached to identical small metal plaques designed to shield us from interstellar dust. On each plaque there's a fanciful diagram indicating that the Sun is our home star. My parents are shown naked on the plaque and my father is waving hello, even though they never spoke much after the divorce.

WE BUY GOLD
\ After *Cría Cuervos* by Carlos Saura \

When I was born, my father wanted to name me Ruskin Marshall, the kind of name that leads to bare-knuckle boxing and haggis-eating competitions. My sister was to be named Mason James. Instead, my mother placed her bets on Michael and Mary. And it was good. Amen.

Fergus came to live with us in the second grade. We called him Fred. He couldn't stop pacing. His arms went crazy sometimes and his hands slapped around and he shouted a lot. He slept in my sleeping bag on the floor next to my bed.

It was my job to get Fred on the bus and take him to class with me, saying that he was my cousin from Canada. His arms and hands flapped all day, and I explained to everyone that Fred was a Rubik's Cube master training for a showdown in Moscow, that he could never stop practicing, calculating, thinking out loud, rotating and clicking the invisible into alignment.

A few nights after he arrived, I awoke to my mother

crying, and to another woman's voice at the door. From my bedroom window I could barely make out my father loading Fred's things into the trunk of a car I'd never seen, his cigarette moving in the dark at his side, like an empty playground swing. And then Fred was gone. And then it was summer.

Last week, when driving my wife to work, I saw him standing near the entrance to a strip mall, twirling a sign that said *We Buy Gold*. I called my mother and she explained that he came from a side of the family I was never allowed to meet, that he and his mother were passing through on their way to San Diego, on the run from her maniac husband, moving from shelter to shelter. They had looked us up in the phone book, my mother said. They eventually had to change their names.

MUTUAL ASSURED DESTRUCTION
\ After *Devilfish* by Jean Painlevé \

I was raised, in part, by my best friend's family. Among
the numerous bonfire-side drunken debates raised by this
group of Jeremiahs (Sr., Jr., and my best friend, III) was
the orbital relationship between the Sun and the Earth.
I was persuaded by Sr. that the kiwi had evolved, in the
span of a few centuries, from mammal to fruit, with the
vestigial hair as empirical evidence of its transformation.
Jr.'s new wife had a series of cassettes whose experts dated
the world at approximately five thousand years. Based on
the ratio of brain to body, Carl Sagan believed that whales
could be our intellectual superiors. The leader of the free
world wanted X-ray-laser-armed satellites in space to blast

the Soviets' missiles. We'll always have Swayze and the Wolverines. The elements of the universe can be seen in a spectrum of bent light. Almonds and peaches share the same stone heart, everything can be represented by ones and zeros, and there's a slow, dark movement in the deep, deep sea.

THE DEEP
\ After *Devilfish* by Jean Painlevé \

In school we learned that the first submersible to reach the ocean floor was connected by a tether to a boat on the surface; they lowered it straight down. When the ball-shaped craft hit bottom, disturbed sediment puffed up in a great cloud and enveloped the windows, which were made from quartz. Lacking windshield wipers, the men inside couldn't see anything more after that point, and when they returned from the deep with tales of weird fishes and other new species glimpsed during their descent, they encountered few believers.

TUNA
\ After *Mon Oncle Antoine* by Claude Jutra \

Everyone was frothing at the mouth for Reagan, and I slept comfortably in the arms of his speeches, beating my tin drum and hoping the Communists stuck their toes over the line. My hometown started getting lots of attention. We'd become the possible retirement destination for the leader of a white supremacist group from northern Idaho. And we were enduring a winter with more rainfall than Bergen, Norway. During the month of November, Norwegian reporters and talking heads from network television affiliates interviewed people we knew about the rain and neo-Nazis in parking lots all over town: Bi-Mart,

K-Mart, the Cenex feed store, labor halls, Gussie's Dine and Dance. Women with big hair and assistants. White vans. Mobile satellite dishes.

Inside our cupboards hung rows of grocery receipts taped up and highlighted. My parents invented a game. On Fridays we'd go over the new receipts—if we'd spent less money on food than the previous week we got to have ice cream for dinner and stay up late and sleep in the living room. All my sister wanted for Christmas was a pair of acid-washed Guess jeans. My father lost his job at Georgia Pacific and took over the shopping duties. At night, lying in bed, I could hear my parents drawing up their strategies for everything. The mortgage, what they could sell, how she might pick up more hours. I also learned that my father found a pair of used Guess jeans at the Goodwill in my sister's size.

By Christmas he had started working a few days a week at the cannery. His rubber boots gleamed and sparkled with fish scales. He stank. To make it look like the jeans were new, my aunt Cheryl, who managed Women's and Juniors at J. C. Penney, put a fake tag through the waistband; my father used one of the vacuum sealers at the cannery to encase the jeans in plastic. When we went back to school after Christmas, my sister wore the jeans every day—they reeked of the cannery. Her teacher asked her to stop wearing them, and she refused. I had to fight everyone who called her "tuna" and got suspended. My mom soaked the jeans in vinegar, scrubbed them with peanut butter, washed them with bleach. At night I ground my teeth and arranged and rearranged the glow-in-the-dark

cosmos on my ceiling. I prayed for the first missiles to hur-
tle through space. I knew whose side I was on.

TOTALLY WATERPROOF
\ After *Mon Oncle Antoine* by Claude Jutra \

Now Christmastime is over, and that means the 6 a.m. slog
up the hill in the snow with my brother to catch the yellow bus to school, with the pop radio station playing Pat
Benatar's "Hell Is for Children" over the crummy speak-
ers. In the dead of winter, Mom places space heaters in
our rooms and Capri-Sun juice boxes with tropical imag-
ery in our metal lunchboxes, mine with its *SPACE 1999*
theme. Meals at home have a theme—what Mom calls
Mexican Night, Italian Night, and Chili Night are varia-
tions on the same ground beef. Along the road to the bus,
we're up to our shins in wet, sloshy January snow, where
in the summer the lilacs die in rank bursts of sweet rot. In
autumn, the woods provide cover for secret military mis-
sions against an occupying army of Fascists having trouble subduing the last pockets of resistance amongst the
hills of southern Wisconsin.

But for now it's not even light yet and we're trudging
in a sulk up that hill for a forty-five-minute ride debat-
ing Reaganomics with the bus driver. At school our boots
sit in dripping little rows in the closet with all the other
kids' waterproof footwear. The boots of kids who get rides
to school in cars with moms who deliver them to houses

with furnaces instead of wood stoves and cupboards filled with food instead of mouse droppings and dead batteries.

Our boots leak, so Mom lines them with plastic bags to keep our toes dry and snug. The best bags to use are bagel bags, because the plastic is thicker and they are elongated, like socks. I brag to everyone about the clever way they keep out the snow, never recognizing that our teachers probably feel sorry for us. This is the school where a group of wild girls will chase me around on the playground in order to pin me down and kiss me on my birthday, the school where I will fail the fourth-grade entry test for the advanced reading group, Cinnamon Peaks, the school where sex education classes will conclude with me believing that a woman's ovaries are located in her breasts, the school where we bob for apples on Halloween and learn about haiku and the intelligence of pigs, and where the principal later will be accused of embezzling from petty cash.

DENIM

\ After *Manufactured Landscapes* by Jennifer Baichwal \

When the school bond measure came up for a vote and didn't pass, all the rural schools were bulldozed and half the elementary and middle schools in the city limits were shut down. Bus services were canceled. Teachers moved. I found myself in a carpool with my friend Brian. His mom drove a beat-up Suburban that often had an alpaca crammed in the far back—it smelled like a barn. As long as I'd known him, Brian had worn black rubber boots to school. He showed the alpaca at the county fair and his mother spun its coat into a fine, thin yarn that she sold on the side of the road along with homemade honey. I'd heard a rumor that all the kids who lived in town wore white hi-tops and Levi's denim jackets. In the dark hours before my first day at the new school I ripped the red Levi's tag from my jeans and sewed it to the front of my USA Olympics windbreaker.

SUPPLY AND DEMAND
\ After *Manufactured Landscapes* by Jennifer Baichwal \

A snapshot taken before we moved out to the country shows my group of friends from the neighborhood, kids with missing teeth and bad futures: a heroin OD, a runaway, a drug dealer, an alcoholic, a settler in the West Bank. In the eastern section of the city, the stink of burnt pig sometimes wafted over from the Oscar Mayer plant. Bullies dangled kids over the befouled river from the bridge near the train tracks and mocked my orthopedic shoes. We had a green Ford Pinto, a car that news reports told us sometimes blew up in rear-end collisions. My mom worked late teaching Lamaze classes to supplement her welfare checks, so I generally took the city bus home by myself from after-school activities. She ironed patches on the knees of my pants when the fabric of the corduroy started wearing thin.

One day I tried to inscribe profane graffiti into the bus's plastic seat, but I only had a pencil to work with.

"How do you spell *blowjob*?" I asked my seatmate, but a passenger overheard and reported me to the driver, who stopped the bus to shout at me. He waited while I slowly erased my writing.

Another day on the bus, this big bearded guy in un-kempt clothes offered to trade shoes with me. His feet were enormous and there was no way my shoes would fit him or his fit me, but I said OK because he scared me. As I removed my ugly clomping shoes, I noticed that he wasn't getting ready to remove his.

"They're orthopedic," I explained. "They reshape the foot. I don't think they would fit anyone else."

"My daughter won't be wearing factory shoes from some sweatshop in Taiwan," he replied.

I handed him my special shoes, hands trembling, and walked the cracked sidewalks home past the bars and the ice-cream factory (which I had always assumed was the world's ideal place to work), ruining my Yoda socks. When my mother heard what happened, she drove me straight to Sears and bought me my first pair of Nikes on credit.

WINTER ACTIVITIES
\ After *Ratcatcher* by Lynne Ramsay \

In my Wisconsin youth I noticed macabre warnings about winter activities. About the ice fishermen who dallied too long in the thaws and unwittingly drove their pick-ups into the bottoms of the lakes. Or snowmobilers who left the assigned trails and got decapitated by barbed-wire fences surrounding the snowy farmlands. You could just freeze, out there on the highway, if your car broke down in a deserted place.

We heated our farmhouse with wood, so we spent the autumn weekends chopping at fallen trunks, bucking the chainsaw through weeping knots, mauling at exhausted stumps, gathering kindling, crumpling newsprint into pitch-tarred barrels that I imagined in the holds of ocean-going ships. Our woodstove kept the mice warm enough in their shivering kitchen cupboards and drawers.

When our house burned down, the county fire chief came out to the site of the embers of our home and declared it the work of a serial arsonist who'd been operating in the area for some time. The accelerant was a two-gallon jug of gas the arsonist had found in our woodshed. All along I had been worried about the wrong catastrophic event.

I wonder now, did anyone or anything ever catch you?

LOTTERY
\ After *Ratcatcher* by Lynne Ramsay \

In the gray, frozen months, the pack rats moved into the garage and ruined everything. Their piss burned through aluminum. They gnawed through air filters and slept in carburetors. We live-trapped them in skunk cages using peanut butter and chicken guts. On Saturday mornings, my father let me empty them into five-gallon buckets half filled with water. He'd sneak me a cigarette and share his thermos of hazelnut coffee. We placed bets on how long it would take. At night we could hear them chisel at the stars. They died with their secrets.

BOXCARS

\ After *George Washington* by David Gordon Green \

Now, the railroad tracks are what I notice most when I return home. Not the tracks themselves, but the absences they carry—no more engines, engineers, noises of boxcars slamming into each other, the angle of early winter light throwing steel shadows across the bay. As a kid, leaning my head against the sweaty passenger-side window of my father's half-ton Chevy, my brothers strapped down under the same seat belt, I would look at the boxcars lined up in the rail yard and think of them as elephants, trunk to tail, making their way through the ancient landscape, the bay like a mirage trailing at their sides. The hitching together, heaving through the entire county full of chips,

logs, beams from Northwest Bridge Company, the stories that belonged to men and women whose bodies were
occasionally freighted from one end of the state to another. Bodies without work permits, addicts, drunk high-
school kids come down from the valley to slum through
the rhythms of the rural American night. Dead bodies,
dumped bodies, bodies alive with fear, bodies of elation,
bodies that should have known better. A one-day notice
in the *Bay River Gazette,* then the ten-mile stretch of industrial waterfront was closed. The dumb fact of it—the
money dried up, the railway shut down, and grass, miles
and miles of grass, began to push its way through gravel
and decades of herbicide, push and push, proud shadows
grown tall and swaying in the wind. The exact weight
of what used to be, what you knew to be true, had come
to rely on, pound per pound and ton per ton, translated
into a negative space of an equal weight sinking into your
chest, like a pylon pushed through layers of muck and silt
down into the bedrock. In the paper, on AM talk radio, at
the State Capitol, the regulators blamed the deregulators,
the state the county, the county the wood beams collaps-
ing in the rail tunnels, the loggers the environmentalists,
and the end-of-days folks blamed our perpetual slipping
from grace.

SELF-ASSEMBLY
\ After *George Washington* by David Gordon Green \

For my birthday, my little brother gave me three dead batteries, which he had wrapped up in a mess of newspaper

and masking tape. My grandfather gave me a self-assembly kit for making a small telescope. When I tried to put the telescope together without adult supervision, I managed to smear glue on the reflector. Everything looked like a greasy thumbprint on a windshield. The first time I used the telescope during the day, I realized the world was up-side-down because I had screwed something in the wrong way around. I used the telescope to spy on my brother as he played with his friends down by the tracks. The inverted image made them float as they passed the soccer ball through the dandelions in the beaten-down parking lot or put their ears to the rails to feel the vibrations before the booming advent of a train. They picked and ate the wild rhubarb that grew along the easement. I was a loner who liked to watch discarded bottles shatter or spin away from the freight cars as they passed. I thought about tying the telescope to the tracks. I started to wonder what would derail a train. A chunk of concrete? Our gas-filled lawnmower? A human body? I snuck through our neighbor's marijuana patch, sniffing the plants that towered over me. I started setting fires, burning little piles of dead leaves, old newspapers, shreds of pornography discovered in an abandoned trailer. A witch with a bulbous shifting face sometimes drifted in the trees outside my bedroom window at night, just watching me. I would aim my telescope past her and watch the surface of the moon, which looked strangely like the skin of a burn victim. The witch didn't look sinister, but I got the sense that she was a little bit concerned about the way I was growing up.

IN THE FORESTS OF THE NIGHT
\ After *For All Mankind* by Al Reinert \

Dwayne became my foster brother right after William "The Fridge" Perry and the Chicago Bears toured the malls and daytime TV shows of America with the "Super Bowl Shuffle." For our ninth birthdays, Dwayne got a ticket to Space Camp and I got a set of fatigues and an Amtrak ticket to visit Ron O'Farrell, my dad's Vietnam buddy who ran a hunting service in Wyoming. My parents always said that Dwayne was blessed.

Ron O'Farrell owned two hundred acres of scrubby land outside Laramie. For ten thousand dollars, you could pay Ron to track a mountain lion, run it up a tree with his hounds, then trap it there until you arrived to shoot it down. Then Ron would take your picture as you knelt over the cat, dogs sitting at attention by your side. The picture would arrive in an aspen frame that Ron put together with small, hand-forged nails. He would stuff and mount the cat himself, then freight it to you.

After trailering the dogs in behind the three-wheelers, we set up camp and slept in a tent for three days while we waited for someone to fly in from Newark. The dogs went mad. The man from Newark was dressed in a wool jacket trimmed with marbled brown leather. He had to choose between a rifle and a compound bow to shoot the cat from ten yards. The mountain lion's eyes glowed when the fire died and the night came out. The dogs never stopped baying, tethered in different spots around the tree, flipping around and pulling wildly at their stakes. The only time the cat moved was when the man shot it in the side with an arrow. It took it a few hours to go limp before it fell to the crunchy alpine duff. Ron slapped the man on the back and shouted, "That's the one," as he released the dogs. That night I drove one of the three-wheelers to a clearing and lit it on fire, hoping that Dwayne could see it as he orbited above.

THINGS THAT DIDN'T HAPPEN
\ After *For All Mankind* by Al Reinert \

So, what if, instead of what really happened, the Apollo 8 spacecraft turned around the curvature of the dark side of the moon to reveal a cargo of dead astronauts? Imagine something went badly wrong on a technical level, but nobody could figure it out. The lifeless ship orbited for several months before crashing down on the surface of the moon. Then the whole lunar program got mothballed. Whenever people on Earth looked up to the sky and saw the moon, they felt the presence of doom and failure.

MILITARY CREASE
\ After *Overlord* by Stuart Cooper \

My father told me that he served in World War II, Korea, and Vietnam, each time with the 101st. I was just big enough to climb into the rafter space in the garage, an unfinished, drafty, detached building whose wide floor planks were rounded at the edges, the wood having soaked up a few generations of motor oil and sawdust. Looking down over the car and the workbench, I popped a screwdriver into the keyhole of a footlocker, broke it open, and removed a neatly folded army dress uniform. I began wearing it to school on Fridays. Each week I added a new medal to the chest and explained its significance. I was surprised, in those next few months, how the uniform grew too small for me, the sleeves landing halfway between my wrists and elbows. My father told me, while showing me some black-and-white photographs of very old buildings with a large mountain range in the background, how poorly he and a few of his buddies did playing soccer against a group of drunk Germans one year during Christmas. Four rifles with bayonets were stuck in the ground for goal posts, and the ball was something one of the men had been making since the first snows had begun to fall.

BUDE
\ After *Overlord* by Stuart Cooper \

During World War II, my maternal grandfather rose through the ranks of the artillery. First he was stationed in Bude, a coastal town in Cornwall, where they fired howitzers at the sea. Then he got shipped off to France, but D-Day had long since passed, and the front moved so quickly that their heavy guns couldn't keep up. He got upgraded to a type of cannon so large that it was fitted to a train car, an impractical, ridiculous, ideal weapon designed to keep my grandfather even safer from harm.

About sixty years later, I read a news item about a cargo ship that sank off the coast in the Atlantic, its million boxes of candy dispersed over the beaches of Britain. Afterward, I started imagining my grandfather back in Bude in 1943, a young man in a dapper green uniform, with a hawklike nose and a wind-burned face, combing the rocks at ebb tide for boxes of sweets and chocolate bars that would not arrive on shore until the next century. Things have reached the point where this false memory is beginning to invade a place in my grandfather's stories about the war. The day will come soon when I begin telling the story the way I see it happening, now, when I close my eyes. He's the first member of his unit to stumble across all that candy; the brightly colored boxes and containers are everywhere.

CROCKETT & TUBBS
\ After *Miami Vice* by Michael Mann \

At first we liked our new stepdad because he put us on the back of his motorcycle. He got hold of a motorless go-cart, a soapbox racer that he would drive in his flatbed truck to the top of the hill where we took turns racing down the lilac-perfumed country road, bailing out, skinning our knees, laughing.

Drug murders on television took place in a neon neverland of speedboats and fast cars that were never red or brown, only black or white. The houses in our area filled up with pot smoke from plants that grew in enormous waves behind the neighbor's barn.

Our stepdad started to become irritable and moody,

pushing us around and helping my ass out the door with his foot. New people started hanging around, like the Vietnam vet with flashbacks who brought his dog out to the farmhouse and shot it back in the fields because it had bitten him.

I had trouble sleeping, and a therapist suggested that I repeat a mantra to myself every night before bed: "Today I was a good boy. Today I did fine."

I turned my green plastic army men toward the bedroom door so that they could shoot anybody who bothered me. An ex-Marine visiting our school said that when Russian missiles hit, papers would burn in wastebaskets thirty miles in every direction, so there was little point in cowering underneath our desks, as the mandatory drills instructed. At this time I was afraid and suspicious of all men in positions of authority. I refused to wear belts; the mere image of a belt hanging on a door hook frightened me.

Sometimes I still had to ride on the back of our stepdad's motorcycle, but I would hold the metal bars behind the seat instead of clinging to his waist like I did before.

My brother and I used to cook up magical potions in secret, using the spice drawer and water, concocting the most disgusting mixtures we could think of: water, cumin, turmeric, cinnamon, oregano. Then we dared each other to drink.

WATER
\ After *Miami Vice* by Michael Mann \

After he got a settlement from a slip-and-fall case against Warehouse Foods, my dad's friend Jack bought a flat-bottom fiberglass speedboat and a storage-unit business on the edge of town. The boat had a metal-flake, root-beer-brown finish. He took fleshy women with loud sun-glasses to the lake on the weekends. He called it his go-fast boat and kept it in one of the storage units.

Before I could legally work, I got an under-the-table job at the do-it-yourself carwash. I unjammed the machine that ate people's quarters, kept the soap reservoirs topped off, used Graffiti-Gone on the swastikas, and refilled the Flying Lasso condom dispenser in the bathroom. Jack would stop by in his truck when I was working and ask how my folks were doing and for a free wash. He prom-ised that he'd let me take the boat to the lake when I was old enough to get my pecker wet. On Tuesday nights he'd gather cardboard from the warehouse dumpsters, grocery stores, and K-Mart, then would soak the load during my Wednesday shift before going to the scale yard at the re-cycle center. He always gave me two Susan B. Anthony dollar coins for using the hose.

The weekend before a meth lab blew the storage unit up and melted the speedboat to its trailer, Jack came by and said he'd like to take me out on the slough to test a slalom ski and some wetsuits he found in one of the units someone had defaulted on. I was sure that, after we put the boat in, we were the only people ever to take a speedboat up the slough. His girlfriend looked like a summertime Juicy Fruit ad with her blond hair sucked back as she skied behind the boat. In a shallow, narrow stretch of water by the dairy farm, Jack yelled, "Get ready," over the deafening wind and motor. He slowed down so that his girlfriend sank back, just the tip of her ski and her head bobbing in the water. He'd pulled her over a place where dead cows were dumped. The headers coming off the engine flared into bugles that had the shimmer of an oily parking lot after a first rain. When she started screaming and crying and begging, he gunned it and pulled her back up into heaven.

12D

\ After *Harlan County USA* by Barbara Kopple \

My mom's boss wore garlic around his neck to ward off vampires. At work, they researched how the mining companies destroyed the American Indian nations who invited them into their lands. "Build universities, build casinos, build opera houses, anything but uranium, or you're fucked forever," that was the basic message. This superstitious man once helped me with a science project that explored extrasensory dimensions beyond our typical conceptions of space and time. Our diagrams postulated that no fewer than five and perhaps as many as twelve dimensions existed. I could picture five to seven dimensions, areas in which the dead lived on perpetually, from which dreams emanated, or through which stray particles traveled between multiple universes that existed side by side without knowing it. But twelve dimensions went beyond my capacity to comprehend. Another thing I failed to understand was, if there could be twelve dimensions, why not fifty-seven? I felt like a liar explaining my theory at the after-school science fair. The teachers said nothing except "interesting," then swiftly moved on to the next project, a bubbling miniature volcano. They must have thought my parents, who weren't there that night, were at home smoking something. But in fact I was just another latchkey kid with divorced parents, this was Reagan's America, and I was a few too many dimensions in over my head. The mining companies were challenged by a dossier of facts about uranium that my mom and her boss transformed into a narrative chamber of horrors. When the companies abruptly withdrew their bids, nobody knew if it was because of the dossier or the garlic or what. But time corkscrewed and split into parallel worlds, just the way my science-fair placards had predicted. The companies returned many years later with the same proposals to dig up the same ground.

COMMUNITY THEATER
\ After *Harlan County USA* by Barbara Kopple \

In the final months of the final layoffs in a terrible decade for the mill, we staged a community production of

Peter Pan at the VFW hall. Before he sold all his tools, Lars loaned us a hydraulic lift that we transformed into a flying machine. The Coast Guard donated a body harness. The shipyard gave us some thin, high-tensile cable.

Later that summer I worked on the crew that dismantled the hall's wooden stage. We planed and milled the planks into tongue-and-groove flooring and sold it all to a high-end contractor from Seattle.

Jenny Maxwell had played Wendy. When hoisted above the miniature London cityscape, she looked like a sick horse raised in a sling, as if being rescued from the floodwaters of a broken levee. The noisy hydraulic lift, placed center stage, shrouded in black bed sheets, drowned out all the dialog, Jenny spinning like a lazy compass needle over all that clear, fine, vertical grain.

NO OUTLET

\ After *Morvern Callar* by Lynne Ramsay \

In the seventh grade, I was rewarded for plagiarizing a short story with a twist ending and kept on writing. But I was never very original. The first thing I wrote by myself took the form of a fake newspaper article about the discovery that plants had feelings. In a future society in which the killing of animals had already been banned, this scientific discovery about plant sentience was a terrible shock. The only possible solution was for people to stop eating other species and start eating each other. In televised spectacles, people were pitted in combat with one another, and the winners ate the losers on live satellite feeds. My first novel, *The Blue Room*, theorized that each person had a series of lives, which they lived one after another. When a person "died," they actually just woke up, and it was the next day of their "real" life. We would have as many lives as a typical person's life had days, around twenty-five thousand lives altogether. None of the adults who read these items laughed in my face or referred me for psychological counseling. Maybe they understood something about gladiators in spandex, secret wars, and extraterrestrial weapons systems named after children's movies. In my play, *No Outlet,* I gradually turned invisible, first to my family, then to the entire world.

TANK MAN

\ After *Morvern Callar* by Lynne Ramsay \

The first time I died was April 13, 1988. In the obituary I included facts from my real life but used a false name, Francis Mulcahy, after the character from *M.A.S.H.* I used my mother's IBM Selectric to type it, then hand-delivered it to the newspaper. I used the local morgue's return address. Francis Mulcahy, devoted son and dreamer. . . . In the dark hours before my parents got out of bed, I had held the note under the dripping faucet in our kitchen. A few fake tears to make it count.

While the cable gods of MTV vibrated through the television tubes of those who lived in the city limits, we were stuck with a monstrous antenna bolted to the side of a fir tree in our backyard. My father sent me up there, in any weather, at all times of the day and night, to make adjustments. We belonged to a telephone party line. Where we lived, if you didn't lie about everything, you at least rounded the edges off the facts. There were always neighbors picking up their phones, hands over the receivers, breathing slowly and quietly in the tunnels of their judgment and curiosity.

The second time I died: June 4, 1989. I was a veteran and a war hero, a widower, a Freemason survived by three loving sons. I used my full name, the real one. For the next two nights, my mother wept and said nothing as a citizen in a white shirt stood in front of a row of advancing Chinese tanks on Chang'an Avenue. He stood there over and over. On every channel. No one knew his name, and I never died again.

THE REVOLUTIONS OF 1989
\ After *Life During Wartime* by Todd Solondz \

The questions were simple. Things like, "Is your house-
hold's annual adjusted gross income over $35,000?" "On
a scale of 1 to 10, with 10 being the most successful, how
would you rate the President's foreign policy over the past
eight years?" "Have you ever purchased a new car?" "If
you had to kill your best friend in order to save the lives
of three strangers, would you do it?" "Coke or Pepsi?"
"Do you think a fetus is a person?" After you took the
test, you were given two free passes to see Dolph Lund-
gren in *Red Scorpion*. The questions were asked in small
cubicles set up in an empty storefront at the mall. The

same space rented out a week at a time to regional Amway symposiums and pitches for time-shares. The hundred answers were allotted a numerical value, and the total score revealed things, within a five percent margin of error, like who would become a sex offender, who would die by self-asphyxiation, and who among us would float back to our cars and have little effect on anything. The scores, corresponding outcomes, and social security numbers were sent to federal law enforcement databases, university researchers, and ad agencies. The mall's parking lot was so full that weekend that cops had to direct traffic. We knew we'd gotten away with something.

BASIC PROGRAMMING
\ After *Life During Wartime* by Todd Solondz \

Instead of Monopoly and Risk, my mom bought "cooperative" board games with titles like Save the Whales. The planet's fate hung in the balance as we confronted imaginary Japanese whalers in our small Greenpeace cardboard motorboats. I saw my dad every other weekend, and he took me to war-gamers' conventions in downtown Milwaukee and Dungeons & Dragons sessions in the suburbs, where hit points bled out under the aegis of cruel demigods in glasses wielding ten-sided dice. Pretty soon I was painting the swords of little elf figurines, and playing Wizardry: Proving Grounds of the Mad Overlord at school on the Apple II+, where goblins lurked in two-dimensional green spaces. My dad snuck me into *Blade Runner* but respected my mom's ban on *Red Dawn* a few years later—I acted out the plot with my friends anyway, but when she saw our plastic weapons in the backyard she said, "Aren't you a little old for that?" One girl in the neighborhood loaned me a copy of an Ayn Rand novel, which my mother quickly confiscated; meanwhile, her parents said she couldn't play with us anymore because Dungeons & Dragons promoted the worship of Satan. We couldn't afford the trumpets and violas my classmates were buying for orchestra practice, but the school computer had killer games like Summer Olympics, featuring the national anthems of the world and the chance to re-create the victory over the Russians in hockey. I brought home artworks made using BASIC programming language and a dot matrix printer. The class I feared the most was home economics. I sometimes skipped that period alto-gether and hid in the library reading puff pieces about the computerized guidance capabilities of the MX missile, which had a "circular error" probable of only one-tenth of a mile and twenty times the power of Hiroshima. After burning my breakfast sandwich and sewing my stuffed basketball inside out, I was in danger of failing home ec, and my parents had somehow convinced me this would keep me from going to high school. The teacher had ru-mors swirling around her about the way she touched the students, but when she called me into her office on the final day of class, she told me I was getting a D and handed me my basketball with the sewing redone so that it showed the right side out. I couldn't decide whether to give the basketball to my dad or my mom, so I kicked it as hard and as far as I could into the woods near the bus stop.

HIS MIND, AFTER THE WAR
\ After *An Autumn Afternoon* by Yasujirō Ozu \

Near the end, the walls in my grandfather's mind began
to fall away to reveal a series of Japanese gardens. Each
morning he moved through the ashy hours until he found
himself walking the edge of a pond, admiring the low
moon, its light like a cable stretched across the calm water. He would see a perfect replica of himself adrift in a
rowboat. From the rowboat he would look back at himself
standing on the shore. Each of him believing the other
lived the false life. Neither could figure out how to attach
himself to the cable of moonlight. They kept a steady eye
on one another throughout the day, tending their separate
gardens, raking the sand into the motions of the Pacific,

each waiting for the other to finally lie down within himself like a chess piece.

GHOST PARTICLES
\ After *An Autumn Afternoon* by Yasujirō Ozu \

When he was dying, my grandfather lost all interest in
the military formalities that had guided his life. He had
been the captain of a submarine that had torpedoed ships
in the Sea of Japan. His brother made admiral and another relative was put in charge of the U.S. naval mission in Antarctica, but my grandfather quit the Pentagon
and spent his later years teaching math at a women's college in Fredericksburg, Virginia, where the graves of the
Union dead covering the hill above the town are lit up
with thousands of candles on Memorial Day.

I remembered how, when his second wife died, my
grandfather carried her ashes in a cardboard box with
the name of a Florida crematory stamped on top through
two airports, metal detector wands, X-ray machines, to
Arlington National Cemetery. He greeted us by saying,
"They didn't give me any trouble."

Five minutes' stroll from the Eternal Flame, he dis-
missed the cardboard salute of an army chaplain, who
spliced together a speech from cue cards. The funeral
took place under a flight path, its heavy roar interrupting
Shakespeare. The box lay on some fake grass in the sun.

But before all that there was the airport motel. He

wanted the paper bag with the box containing the ashes placed near the bed. The room was still, like all motels, except the ice machine woke us in the night. The room next door had no number; it had been effaced or removed.

And when he died, we buried my grandfather in the same place, and there received the folded flag after a horse-carriage cortege—he'd won the Navy Cross. One time, back in the Pacific, Japanese sonar had detected the ship and started depth-charging his sub because someone forgot to put a rubber band around a loose drawer, which clattered to the floor. My grandfather took the sub below its test depth and the hull withstood the pressure.

"I was twenty-three," he explained, when I asked him about it. "They put us in charge because they knew older men wouldn't take so many risks."

But when he had been very ill, he didn't talk about the war. He wanted ice cream. He wanted to eat raspberry jam straight from the spoon. His retirement condo looked out over an inlet from the Gulf of Mexico where his little fishing boat rested at a mooring place that attracted dolphins and pelicans. He had tumors in his lungs and his brain, and he wanted them treated aggressively even though his time was short. He asked me to play "The Girl from Ipanema" on his CD player over and over again. He secretly requested a tiny splash of good scotch in his ice water after dinner, "just for the taste."

CONCORDAT
\ After *Burden of Dreams* by Les Blank \

I got my license when I was sixteen and drove myself every Wednesday to Young Life, an evangelical youth ministry, where we were at war with the agents of the Antichrist. I discovered that Jesus wanted me to pay for and attend a summer retreat in the woods of Northern California, where I was to join a group of high school boys that would, for two weeks, carry fifty-foot segments of twelve-inch mainline irrigation pipe up a mountain trail passable only by donkey. I was called, so I listened. Jason, our expedition leader, was a college freshman who dressed in fatigues and combat boots. He taught us the lyrics to "White Minority." We sang as we worked. We were rednecks from dead industrial towns, inner-city kids, and suburban misfits. Jason reminded us that we were God's soldiers, all in equal standing with the Lord, called to carry pipe. We were going to bring water to the desert. We would topple Pharaoh's army. In another country, in another war, one of our hands attached the wire to Bonhoeffer's neck.

THE HILL
\ After *Burden of Dreams* by Les Blank \

After my mom's third divorce, a family friend, Howard, hired me for summer. Manual labor around his basement and backyard. For a week straight I sorted through thousands of his nails and screws, ordering them by sizes and functions into tiny plastic boxes. Then came a truly medieval task. Howard had a slight rise in his yard—he called it The Hill, even though the hump was no more than a foot or so in elevation. What he wanted me to do was flatten The Hill by hand. Just dig up the dirt and move it around until it was more or less level. A pick, a pitchfork, a tape-measure, and a shovel. Third World work in the sun. Howard would appear three times each day, first with iced tea, then later with sandwiches, and again at 3 p.m. with a Diet Coke. Weeks later, I looked over The Hill and saw that I had chipped away about half of the thing. I dreamed of finding gold coins or ring-bearing skeletons buried inside, but there were only worms. Our next project was a little blue junker Ford Fiesta with a stench of gas about it, a rusty car Howard found somewhere and was trying to fix up. We replaced the exhaust intake and the fuel pump out of junkyard parts. He dragged me all over the city, tasking me with comparing prices and haggling with staring men in ripped T-shirts, scavenging wrecks and diving in with wrenches while dogs shrieked in deserted lots nearby. When the car was working again, Howard taught me how to drive the stick shift, drowning out the grinding gears with opera broadcasts from public radio. One day near the end of the summer, he gave me a box of his old tools and told me to put them in the trunk. Then he handed me the keys, saying the car was now my problem.

VAMPIRE RADIO

\ After *Border Radio* by Allison Anders,
Dean Lent, and Kurt Voss \

The first punk show I recorded off the local underground radio station was a Halloween special devoted entirely to songs about serial killers. A local band croaked on about Satanic blood drinkers in the state asylum or something along those lines. By this point I had quit varsity soccer and I was smoking a lot of weed in my friend's mom's trailer down the block. The friend had been to court for trashing a weather station with an axe.

"That thing had it coming," he said. Then we watched *Return of the Living Dead* again, or *Martin*, a movie about a deranged kid who believes that he is a vampire.

My friend's older sister began screwing the hell out of me when I turned sixteen. It started when she was visiting home on holidays from college and continued after she graduated. A secret education began: clove cigarettes, German philosophy, oral sex, French press coffee, incense, films with subtitles—the usual. Much later, when I finally broke it off with her, on New Year's Eve, she bit me.

"There," she said, admiring the bruise and the white indentations of her teeth.

There weren't any punks or goths in my suburb, but the school did have a machine in the basement underneath the basketball court in the gym that drained the life out of the town's youth. A guy with a pet ferret and a long black trench coat befriended me after I had checked out of the magic social circles of the sports teams, the Midwestern cliques of these children of the corn. He wrote wonderful horror stories like "The Leech," in which a monstrous lake creature terrorized people who resembled our classmates. I wrote vampire stories in which vampires were, like, a metaphor for capitalist exploitation. . . ? He distracted the librarian's assistant while I stuffed *The Complete Stories of Edgar Allan Poe* into my backpack.

"Everyone thought you were on heroin," my kid brother revealed later on. That was the rumor going around about my nocturnal pallor. In fact, I was spiritually ruined by spending the night with my friend's older sister. My mom found a red pill on the floor of my trashed bedroom and told me she'd had it sent to a lab for chemical analysis. It must have been cough medicine, but it came back labeled as speed. I wanted to sleep all day long, I reasoned with her, so how could I be a speed freak?

I should confess that all of these things happened after some childhood friends of mine got killed in a car accident. They were on their way home from an away game in a farm town. It happened during the first snowfall of the year, when another driver crossed over into their lane. I had lost touch with them in junior high, when organized sports had lured me in through peer pressure. A month or two before they died, I had made a plan to hang out with them and play Dungeons & Dragons, for old time's sake, but we never made it happen. Back in the old days, it didn't seem possible that any of the elfin personas we had carefully endowed with dexterity and intelligence and charisma bonuses could ever run out of hit points or spells. Our loaded dice existed to be rerolled; again and again we rose from the dead.

RENTED SHOES
\ After *Border Radio* by Allison Anders,
Dean Lent, and Kurt Voss \

Before it was a sad place to get laid or get your teeth kicked out, and long before it was torn to the ground and replaced by a Dollar Store, I spent my time at the combo bowling alley–roller rink. Jessica's dad owned Bayside Lanes and Rollerdome, and we bowled and skated for free in trade for spraying Lysol into the rental shoes and skates. We

also stockpiled the expired cigarette packs from the vend-
ing machines in the lounge, mostly Benson and Hedges
Light 100s, which we sold at school. Our friends and ene-
mies smelled like fast-burning menthol. I don't remember
why, but Jessica and I made a pact to lie about everything
for an entire year. We got the idea from a movie. I can't re-
call the name of it, but I know it featured talking dogs and
an actor who played Soviet villains. We started by saying
that we stole the cigarettes from the patients in a nursing home, where we also claimed to be orderlies and wit-
nesses of supreme cruelties. We lied about all the drugs
we slammed into our veins, all the things we ripped off,
all the people we screwed in other towns, the revenges we
took for money that was owed us, how we got chased off
the reservation, how we drove to the border to pick up
five pounds of "Mexi-shake." The summer before Jessica
went missing from a cannery in Alaska, she gave me a tat-
too of a question mark on my right shoulder using a red
ballpoint pen and a sewing needle. I have powers. I can
undo everything and take myself back to the empty lanes,
the last drunks having just stumbled out, the cops gone,
"Hotel California" quiet, forgivenesses given or taken, the
money counted, bartender tipped out, the shoes sprayed
and bathrooms bleached, the double doors locking the
night out and us in, the black lights making our lips shine
after we coated them in cue chalk from the pool tables,
the Angel of Death tossed in the dumpster, the Dead Ken-
nedys filling up our mix tapes, and us, ready to raise the
curtains and invent what comes next.

MEANINGLESS INTENSIFIERS
\ After *Donnie Darko* by Richard Kelly \

A girl from school called you up long distance and asked
you to measure your dick for her while you were on the
phone, promising to keep the information secret. You took
the long phone cord into your room and gave her an answer—and that was how it started. A friend of hers who
wore blue-jean miniskirts and wet black eye makeup
would put her bare knees right up against yours under the
desk during partner projects. Another explained that after school her parents would be away for, like, hours, and
by the way she had gotten hold of some schnapps. Their
clique would lower their glasses when they glimpsed you
across the classroom, pass by in a laughing trio, ask if you

were going to the game later, offer you a ride home, and hold out candy, like creepy old men.

The girl with the schnapps asked you for some advice about relationships, like the one she was having with a friend of yours. Could you meet somewhere to discuss it? You didn't call up your friend and ask if this was OK before saying yes because you sort of knew this was not OK. When she picked you up, she looked splendid as a fake blonde in braids with fake pearls and fake tan in a sports car with new car smell, wearing short shorts, her mother's too-large high heels, and a flimsy blue sweater, despite the hot weather, a pack of menthols and Breathsavers and flavored condoms on the dashboard. The schnapps sat between you in the cup holder, badly disguised in a brown paper lunch bag.

"Is this your parents' car?" you said, stupidly, thinking this was where life ended in certain areas of the Midwest.

"My mom's," she said. "They're divorced. She's away fucking at the lake this weekend. So I stole the car and I'm not wearing any underwear."

"What about _____?" you said, mentioning your friend, her boyfriend.

"I want to *see* it," she said. "Word is out."

"I might have exaggerated," you said. "A little."

"We'll find out," she said. "I brought a measuring tape."

She drove to a secluded section of winding country highway outside of town. It was more or less the same spot where some friends of yours had died in a head-on collision with a drunk driver about a year earlier.

"Don't you know what happened out here?" you said.

"Yes," she said, unbuttoning her sweater.

"Wait a minute," you said.

"Oh, I get it now," she said. "You fucking lied."

She was so furious driving home that she downed the schnapps and nearly smashed the car on one of the sharp curves. To punish you she left her sweater magnificently unbuttoned all the way back to town. She told you what she would tell her boyfriend about what you had supposedly tried on her. All the while you thought about the girl you really wanted to date, who just that week had given you a cassette tape of her viola recital, glorious in its imperfections.

THE LANGUAGE OF THE AFTERNOON
\ After *Donnie Darko* by Richard Kelly \

When you date a dying person, things can get pretty exciting. At the time, Stephanie was deep into the Gnostic Gospels. It was all about a parallel existence, the hand of God moving beside us the way mountain lions crept in the shadows beside joggers in college towns. Stephanie's illness gave her a wonderful, frank demeanor. I met her the summer after I graduated. We were both working the weekend shift at Subway. Our shift manager was named Scottie. He wanted us to call him Pippen. The first time we worked together, she said, "Do you want to quit on our lunch break and go screw?"

Her doctors gave her a seize-the-day prognosis, and we

talked a lot about our parallel selves: how they went to college, grew apart, broke up, lost touch, moved to different states, and ran into each other at a sales conference in a Las Vegas hotel bar. How they laughed, burned their stiff corporate clothes in the parking garage, and made love against an airport shuttle. . . .

For whatever reason, talking about the parallel world made us drift apart until we eventually grew to resent one another. She moved up north to be close to her doctors and treatments, and I stayed in town and worked some crummy jobs. When she moved, she didn't ask me to come with her or to keep in touch or to visit.

Last week, I ran into her when I was on a vacation/business trip in Sacramento with my wife and our two adopted kids. I don't know why I canceled one of my daytime meetings and met Stephanie in secret at a hip outdoor bistro. We drank, laughed, made fun of how fat I'd become. High above us was a billboard featuring a woman with two dolphins for lips who balanced a cruise ship on her bright blue forehead. Three motorcycle cops huddled together in the shade, the white tops of their helmets bobbing like seagulls. A hot day during a serious drought. Stephanie, whom I had spoken ill of so many times, told me that she had lived eight years longer than any other survivor of her particular illness, the name of which, if you say over and over, starts to sound like "the language of the afternoon." The heat poured up from the street like an invisible waterfall running backwards, which became, for a moment, visible for the first time.

SHEETS OF GALAXIES
\ After *Intergalactic* by Nathanial Hörnblowér \

For a while my family thought I was interested in science, when in fact I only loved space. The aspirational Christmas gift of Stephen Hawking's *A Brief History of Time* lay dumped in a corner of my bedroom floor, abandoned at the very first equation. My mother sent me to some kind of high achiever's summer session in astronomy, something she clearly could not afford. The teacher handed out photocopies of a page filled with dots.

"Look closer," he said.

Each dot was actually a galaxy. These tiny thumbprint whorls filled the paper. He had given us a sheet of galaxies from the deep fields of space. I fell in love with that piece of paper.

In science class, I hypothesized about dark energy and failed the math sections of the tests. My extra-credit essay, designed to save my grades for college, explored the concept that there might be extra universes we could not see on the other sides of black holes—our own universe "was only the start of what lightless infinite space might contain."

"If there are other worlds and other galaxies," I wrote, "then why not other universes?"

"What If!?!," the teacher wrote in red ink next to a giant C−. And then: "SEE ME after class."

As it turned out, I had nothing to fear—the teacher only wanted to loan me a paperback novel called *In Watermelon Sugar*. I had told him early on that I wanted to be an astronaut or an astronomer, and this was his way of letting me down gently.

THROWN ROD, CRUEL STARS
\ After *Intergalactic* by Nathanial Hörnblowér \

After their seventeen-year-old son Mikey was killed in a car crash, all Steve and Deb Carson (our neighbors of ten years) talked about were Satanic barcode scanners at the grocery store, the secret societies American presidents belonged to, and false cryptoscientific work trumping the efforts of true cryptoscience.

For the entire month of December, after her International Scout blew a rod, I gave Deb a ride to the Lazy-J Motor Lodge, where she worked nights cleaning rooms. It was a particularly brutal winter, and we all got tired of the weatherman telling us how many records were broken. Even the stars seemed cruel. On our trips together, Deb confided in me her deepest anxieties about the CIA and the Jewish media. The last time I gave her a ride to work, the unmistakable shape of a man's face appeared on the inside of my windshield. It stayed there for all fifteen miles of our ride, and I looked through the space where his eyes were, trying to keep track of the road as it disappeared in the fog. She gave me chance after chance, but all I could say was, Have a good one, See you soon, Take good care.

PULP FICTION
\ After *Coup de Torchon* by Bertrand Tavernier \

After I ditched sports in high school, I started staying home so that I could catch up on my reading and wait around to see if Rachel could break away from her job and her boyfriend to have sex with me. I got heavily into noir with infidelity themes, where life broke you in a rat trap and love led down a steep path to murder and insurance fraud. Rachel wasn't like the girls in my classes; she had graduated from college and she talked liked those doomed women who left lipstick on cigarettes, dyed black hair on pillowcases, blood in the alleys.

"He'd never stop puking if he found out half the things I've done," she said.

Then she committed more statutory crimes on my body, or teased me with hints and stories about other lovers, and joy flooded into my life for the first time in many years. I racked up forty absences in my senior year, and wrote a term paper on the meaning of psychopaths in the novels of Jim Thompson.

"Why do you like this garbage?" My English teacher wrote on the paper in red ink.

The liars, cheats, chiselers, salesmen, murderesses. The highways, flimsy motels, diners, and crime scenes. Rachel's boyfriend should have had me killed, but instead he seemed bemused by my willingness to hang around and lie through my teeth. No sap, he showed me *Blood Simple,* in which the lover dies horribly, and then watched me watching the death and mayhem.

For a long time afterward, I kept waiting for the other shoe to drop, but I never got shot, stabbed, blown up, thrown from a train, garroted, poisoned, or beaten down. That will occur at the proper place and time in the future, I'm sure, everything according to plan.

THE WATCH
\ After *Coup de Torchon* by Bertrand Tavernier \

Someday, I will buy myself a watch at an airport duty-free kiosk in Denver to celebrate securing a deal for 250,000 units with a defense contractor. The watch will be Danish. Its woven titanium band will be like a rope

lowered halfway into hell then pulled back up before anyone down there can see it. When I open my briefcase of
samples, what you'll really be seeing is a map of Denmark,
and I will be the King of Denmark. I will make my people
celebrate me. My seven wives will wave at my side. Everyone will fall into line. I will command my generals to take
no prisoners and do what they will with the citizens. My
watch will strut around eating a greasy drumstick. It will
make bribes and take bribes and acquire more land. It
will show up to parties drunk and go home with a beautiful young woman to grunt into. At night it will sleep next
to me. When I press my ear to its smooth quartz face, I
will hear ten days of rain ticking down through the trees,
making the members of a search party miserable. They've
been out in the woods calling a child's name. They've
held hands and combed every inch of the land. The dogs
and helicopters turned up nothing. The last members
of the search party have stripped off their ponchos, the
dim flashlights clenched between their knees. They drive
home to their separate houses and feel ashamed. But the
way the watch will tell the story is incredible, like a star
ready to collapse and suck in all the light around it. It will
know where the body's hidden and promise to tell me.

MOM'S MORPHINE
\ After *Jesus' Son* by Alison Maclean \

I once came into a bottle of pure liquid morphine, a memento from my mom's double hip replacement, which was not a success and led to her catastrophic depression. When I couldn't find a summer job after my junior year of high school, I experimented with the stuff for a while. After adding more morphine at bedtime, I began seeing dark little things scurrying around the apartment from the corner of my eye.

Voices started talking to me.

They said things like:

"We're going to kill you and make it look like an accident!"

"Why?" I said, very loudly and distinctly, trying to drive off the darkness.

"Oh, your crimes," they said.

Obviously the thing to do was pour the bottle down the sink, but you weren't supposed to do that, because the drug would enter the water supply. So I put the bottle into a bag and hid it in the trunk of the car. I wasn't willing to get rid of the stuff, and sometimes I would retrieve the bottle in the dead of night for more séances. My body went deliciously numb and I stared at my feet for fun, while my brain unleashed its full firepower against itself. When you're starting off on liquid morphine, you can take it with a dropper in water or on a spoon and lick the spoon. I would drive around with the bottle in the trunk like a felon delivering a package, which made the days seem full of interest and the suburbs worth noticing.

Finally, at Christmas, I drove to the hospital that had botched my mother's case and dumped the rest of the morphine into a planter, right on top of a flowering evergreen that had never done anything except try to cheer up the frozen entrance to an emergency waiting room.

BOYS
\ After *Jesus' Son* by Alison Maclean \

I dropped out of high school and studied for my GED at Tidewater Tech, as it was unaffectionately called. I worked odd hours filling frozen meat orders at a local wholesaler. My closest friend, Zig, delivered prescription drugs in his '83 Blazer for the Spouse-Reitz pharmacy, the five-and-dime by the fabric store. He'd pick me up after work on Tuesdays and take me on his final run, the Sea Grove Trailer Park, where Christopher lived, if you could call it living. His illness was advanced and made it impossible to guess his age—he had hairless legs, veins that ran in tight, jagged patterns, swollen ankles. As far as we could tell, he wore a bathrobe all day, watching *Days of Our Lives, All My Children,* and *Oprah,* eating food delivered by Meals on Wheels and the Lions Club. Zig had thin blond hair, hair that didn't seem real, that hung past his ears, river water pouring over a smooth rock. Christopher gave us a mix of pills and tall, sweaty cans of Coors wrapped in McDonald's napkins, and the three of us sat on the couch. The shore wind rocked the trailer, the half-light danced on the wings and legs of the glass figurines that piled up in my head, and Christopher twirled the hair behind Zig's ear, taking deliberate, shallow breaths, saying, "Boys, boys," as we all climbed the ladder of those moments up into something that floated over the town and tore itself open on the branches of the scrubby pines that lean toward the sea.

SMALLER THAN A DOLLAR
\ After *Salesman* by Albert Maysles,
  David Maysles, and Charlotte Zwerin \

Between high school graduation and college I worked at a
popular gas station. Diane Neely, a girl I'd thought about
since forever, walked in one day and started laughing
when she saw me there at the register in my red polyester
shirt by the Big Gulp promotional display with my stupid
grim smile and my HELLO nametag.

"I'm sorry," she said. "But . . . you? Really?"

I drove a rusted-out Ford Fiesta with suspect brakes.
It was the late 1980s. I listened to the Misfits sing "She"
and used the emergency brake (or sometimes a snowbank)

to help stop the car. The whole thing was a lot like what Keats said about a thing of beauty.

Earlier, when school was still in session, I had driven another girl home after she whispered something in my ear: "Do you know what fucks like a tiger and winks?" And then she winked. She, a sleek track star, and I, captain of the tennis team—an honor which, in our town, only meant that I had turned up for all the matches.

But I had fallen far from glory, and at the convenience store that summer, I sold gas, lottery tickets, and milk-in-a-bag. That was the thing everyone wanted, milk-in-a-bag, bladder after bladder of carry-out plastic udders. Once I came in at 5 a.m. to help unload the delivery truck, making a point of displaying total ineptitude. I closed the store by myself after they got to trust me—I only stole minor items like individual packs of Pall Malls ("Wherever Particular People Congregate," the label read). I didn't take entire cartons like some people. I checked the gas levels with a great wooden stick featuring twenty feet of notches—an artifact that could be displayed one day as a quasi-religious relic in a museum dedicated to the era of cheap petroleum. Calm transported the parking lot at closing time, when I signaled to helpless motorists trying to gas up after the pumps and the lights had been shut off. They would look back at me as if I were a minor god of shrugs. During the day I enjoyed helping customers break down their food stamps into change through many tiny purchases, then amalgamate the coins into larger sums for scratch-off lottery tickets. They couldn't buy prepared food with the stamps. They bought milk-in-a-bag and other small items that would give them ninety cents back in change, leave the store, then come back and repeat the process. Then they would lose the lottery, or they would win the lottery and spend all the winnings on more lottery tickets, until every cent they had was gone. We had their cash, their candy wrappers, and their trashed game cards.

"You should work on your smile," my manager said. But I had bad teeth.

Alone late at night I would stare at the open safe behind the register stuffed with vast rolls of lottery tickets, trying to figure out a way to steal them all and not get caught. I had my chance at ruin and jail, another tangent life, and again and again, night after night, I failed to act.

INVENTING THE HOURS
\ After *Salesman* by Albert Maysles,
David Maysles, and Charlotte Zwerin \

Once, at four in the morning, with a good spot in line outside the Westland Free Clinic, I saw a job posting on their community bulletin board: "Be your own boss. Invent your own hours." The doctor who saw me for my pneumonia wore dirty white hi-tops and greeted me with, "We don't do venereal diseases, so I hope you're not about to drop your pants."

As it turns out, I was qualified to be an Associate Team Member for a door-to-door cutlery company. In just one hour I was trained to stand in strangers' doorways, to cut through a running shoe with a bread knife, a mooring rope with a six-inch chef's blade. These were the days when I used to dress like a Mormon missionary and let strangers convert me. I would drink coffee for a dollar, smoke a cigarette for five, and, if lucky, renounce the Prophets while touching the breasts of housewives.

I moved from one week to the next with the humiliating confidence that God reserves for the poor. Brother Knife, there's no middleman between you and me and eternity.

SELF-PORTRAIT WITH PLANTAIN
\ After *Something's Got to Give* by
  Ari Marcopoulos and The Beastie Boys \

While shopping for my little sister's sixteenth birthday at
the Salvation Army, I found a pewter miniature of the Eif-
fel Tower. It had one broken leg. I hung it from my truck's
rearview mirror with some baling wire I kept behind my
seat. At the tower's base was a tiny engraved plaque that
said *Victory Cruiselines 1991* in calligraphic script. In the
checkout line I decided I'd move to the valley and go to
college.

"You're going to love the ethnic food," my friend Suzan
had told me earlier that year, while home for Christmas
break. She'd spent the semester working out the details

for staging an adaptation of *Sexual Perversity in Chicago* in an empty swimming pool near the campus. "And the coffee," she said, "oh my God, the coffee."

My boss Gary said, "College is a great place to meet homos," running a file across the chisel-teeth of his chainsaw.

"I'm sick of working in the rain," I said.

"You won't last a month," he said, and punched me in the arm a little harder than usual.

That first afternoon in the valley was hot and humid. I stopped at a health food co-op and bought what I thought to be a banana. I sat on my tailgate and peeled at my lunch, using my truck keys to dig through the stringy layers of tough skin. The fruit had a bitter starchiness to it and was impossible to chew. I threw it away.

Earlier that day I'd pulled off the highway near the edge of my hometown to take a ceremonial last look at my old life. Green Ridge, the most visible from that side of town, had recently been clear-cut. I'd been sneaking up there for a few weeks, drinking and shooting clay pigeons with a couple of buddies. We managed to haul off several pickup-loads of good wood from the slash piles. I split it into firewood, sold it, and made enough to pay for a tune-up and my first month's rent.

As I idled on the side of the road, my birthplace rising up before me with its mills and bridges, with its stoplights that blinked yellow after 10 p.m., I tried to feel profound, my truck loaded with all my possessions, a little daylight coming up through the rusty holes in the floor, but nothing happened. Later, a logging plane dropped napalm on Green Ridge, and it smoldered into the night.

GET PAID TO READ BOOKS!
\ After *Something's Got to Give* by
Ari Marcopoulos and The Beastie Boys \

The magazine ad said I could get paid to read books if I called a certain phone number.

"Is it OK if I'm underage?" I asked.

"As long as you have the $19.95," a woman's voice informed me.

"I don't!"

"Don't worry," she said. "We're willing to bill you."

Then my writing was accepted, with a glowing letter of praise, for *Breakout*, an anthology of soon-to-be-famous poets from my local area, but the publishing company wanted a modest fee for printing costs. I was really on a roll. When I asked my mom for the money for these ventures, she broke it down for me.

"They pay you," she said, "once you're good enough. Capitalism is ascendant, dear."

I wept bitterly listening to "Fight The Power" on cassette, then ordered the items anyway. When they arrived, I refused to pay, but I also never opened the packages to discover their secrets of success. The TV reran *Images of the Decade*: Alaskan birds dripping with thick black oil from the *Valdez* disaster, clouds shaped by the explosion of the Space Shuttle *Challenger*, the fall of the Eastern Bloc, bombers rusting in the desert by the dozens. I took a golf club to an empty refrigerator box, slicing it up into pieces. Then I took the pieces out to the woods, set them on fire, and added the poetry anthology and the how-to pamphlet to the blaze, squirting lighter fluid from our barbecue set over the heap. I fed my poem—the only copy, handwritten—to the fire. Then I sprayed the lighter fluid in a figure eight around the bases of two tiny flowering bushes and watched their leaves and yellow petals soften and then crumble into the flames. Finally, using the last of the lighter fluid as a flammable guide, I led the fire to the base of a small poplar tree, but it wouldn't catch.

SPACETIME

\ After *Puce Moment* by Kenneth Anger \

Regular as clockwork, this guy used to come into the discount bookstore where I worked after my community college plans fell through. I had been caught skateboarding on the steps of the federal building downtown—running away from the agents after they had drawn their guns had been unwise. I looked forward to seeing this guy at the bookstore because he was friendly to me and because it intrigued me that the only things he ever bought were outdated travel guides to European cities. One week it would be Prague, the next week Budapest or Venice.

He didn't exactly look like the globetrotting type. Actually, he kind of slobbered, counting out his change with infinite care, one coin at a time, after you handed him his Fodor's *Barcelona*.

I couldn't help picturing him in his room, wherever it was, with all these books and maps, poring over descriptions of the Musée d'Orsay or the Campidoglio. Who was I to say that, inside that room, there wasn't a hidden wormhole in the fabric of space that led him out into the immense turquoise vistas of Amalfi or the windy hills around Edinburgh Castle?

Our customers, instead of asking him for advice on decent restaurants near the British Museum, narrowed their eyes at him, putting on that look which pretends, instead of looking away, to see nothing at all.

TEMP
\ After *Puce Moment* by Kenneth Anger \

I was just old enough to have fantasies about driving across the country. Getting high and drunk, going skinny dipping with strangers and college girls, maybe get some barbed wire inked around my bicep. It was plausible. I had an '84 Vanagon with a new transaxle and a little money saved from some dirt bikes I'd rebuilt and sold. None of my friends were in jail yet. None of them had died from amphetamines or suicide or had moved across the county line and into the ether of other towns. I lived in a little window. But then I paid my life's savings to the

County after I got arrested for some petty theft and entered the world of temp agencies. A month in Georgia Pacific Veneer doing putty patch. A few weeks roofing a low-income housing development. Cement work. More mill work. I put in a request to be moved to something indoors and easy.

"Like a secretary?" my handler asked. "You don't have the tits for it."

I got placed in Ace Dry Cleaning and Tailoring, which was run by Charles and Tony. They lived in the apartment above the store in a building that used to serve as an annex to the Oddfellows Hall next door. They were high enough to have a view of the bay, high enough that Gucci's Italian restaurant and the sad row of main street shops disappeared from view altogether.

For a few months I steamed sport coats, assisted on simple tailoring jobs, but mostly worked the counter. It didn't take me long to realize that Charles and Tony were shut-ins. They hired temp workers as a way to meet new people. I made their bank deposits and did their grocery shopping on the clock. Tony wore the exquisite pencil moustache of an aristocrat. When Charles played show tunes and sang along, Tony would look at me in a huff and roll his eyes. After I spent nearly six months at the Ace, we started rehearsing a three-man version of *Lysistrata*. For costumes, we dressed ourselves in clothes that belonged to our town's powerful women: the mayor, a councilwoman, doctors, the lumber baron's wife. We performed our play for a small group of Charles and Tony's friends, then they let me go.

AT THE REST STOP, AN HOUR SOUTH OF THE STATE PRISON, INTERSTATE 5

\ After *Vagabond* by Agnès Varda \

The woman has the hood of her '85 Jimmy propped up with a white aluminum curtain rod. She only has forty-five minutes, she tells me, before visiting hours are over. There's not enough time to let the engine cool. There's no way to remove the radiator cap. Even when I use my shop rags and work gloves. The antifreeze begins to smell good in the sunlight.

For the last hour I've been listening to a radio show about famous art thieves. Marcel, the thief known only by one name, was caught, finally, just last year. During his trial, he wept, explaining that his favorite piece, a

Marc Chagall sketch of a woman floating across a night sky, was legitimately his, and that he would kill himself if his children weren't allowed to keep it.

She's looking at me, as if I'm thinking, *You asked for this . . . I told you from the beginning . . . You had it coming.*

I'm looking down at her blue Nikes, which have never been closer to the ground.

The sketch, Marcel explained to the jury, had once belonged to his father, who had fought the Germans in the snow.

YURI GAGARIN EXPLORES OUTER SPACE
\ After *Vagabond* by Agnès Varda \

When she discovered the little bottle of morphine—the secret stash under the kitchen sink that I had lied about throwing away—she was so angry that she took off her work shoes and threw them at me, one after the other, the second one clonking off the back of my head and clattering into the unwashed dishes. She unfolded her knife and stabbed the bottle on the counter as if the poor thing were a possessed child's toy in a horror movie. Then she tried to set fire to it with her Zippo, leaving a mangled and melted heap, while screaming, "Happy Birthday!" It was like watching someone burn down a forest or kill a kitten. Her lovely blonde hair kept bobbing close to the flame, and I was afraid she would set herself on fire. When she fled the house in heels without her coat or her cigarettes, giving me an hour to pack and clear out for good, I licked some of the liquid morphine off of the burnt plastic and scraped the remnants of the little pool into a travel-sized shampoo bottle for the road. Then I grabbed my sleeping bag and my collection of NASA commemorative Space Shuttle decals and stole her cigarettes and her folding knife. I put on my winter ski hat with the white pom-pom at the top, and headed out into the snow.

It isn't much fun to celebrate your nineteenth birthday in a broken-down city without a job or any place to sleep in the winter, but how could I blame anyone but myself? I was trash and I knew it. I knew an area of the city where some of the mansions built for robber barons were now deserted, and the private tennis courts displayed signs advertising VACANT LAND. The foreclosed squatters and the broke students and the homeless and the drug gangs and the police and the ghosts of the city's splendid past existed in parallel universes, seeing right through one another.

I thought the building was empty until I found a kid my own age in a red scarf and a soaked hoodie smeared with mud shivering next to a cold fireplace in the grand, empty parlor of a condemned house surrounded by warning signs and fences. While he watched me silently and mice raced around the edges of the great room, I draped my sleeping bag around his shoulders and started attacking the boarded-up windows for firewood, breaking the plywood apart with an art deco wrought-iron poker from a matching set of implements by the fireplace. I took a wad of toilet paper from my back pocket and lit a fire under some wood splinters, at which point the room started filling up with smoke.

"You have to open the flue," he said. "Don't you know anything?"

"It's my birthday," I said. "I have some morphine."

"As Yuri Gagarin once put it, 'Let's go!'" he said.

A fire started to draw, and we shared the sleeping bag, close enough to the fire to feel as though our faces were getting sunburned. I dismantled the remains of some classic chairs and took apart the rotten ornamental staircase for fuel. The place had already been stripped several times for plumbing fixtures and copper pipes. Outside, glimpsed through the diamond shapes of the leaded windows, the snow drifted down lazily in the streetlamps. We took the last of the morphine and played a game where we described the snow: "It looks kinda like sparks . . . no, fireflies . . . or feathers maybe. . . ?"

THE END
\ After *The Element of Crime* by Lars von Trier \

For two dollars you can watch the world ending on a city bus. The electric-powered bus shudders on its clumsy wires through winter floods, collecting huddled and broken people, transferring old folks and crazies from shelter to hospital. Anyone who is fundamentally fucked rides for free, entrance through the back door, no questions asked, just don't stab anyone. It takes forty minutes for the bus to move three miles. The rich pass overhead in space cars, hovercraft, floating rooms complete with carpets, cats, pastel flowers in vases, wireless stock-trading platforms and transparent retractable domes. The hovercraft are charged up with private Tesla coils that tower over the city, sparking out into the lake fog and sometimes zapping the buses dead for a minute or two with their rolling shimmer of light and static. As the bus rolls through my district, I see that gang rule has been restored and that the community college campus has completed its transformation into a "sex positive" entrepreneurial entertainment zone. Illegals line up around the block in the downpour outside the satellite consulate of Costa Rica next to the Niketown. Plastic shopping bags have been banned; possession is a felony. My paper grocery bags have melted in the rain, I'm hoisting up what looks like wet trash I'm planning to eat later. Getting soaked on my way from the bus stop to my apartment entrance, I see blood washing down the sidewalk on my block and families sleeping in storefronts during business hours. At night the rattling of shopping carts wakes me. I'm expecting the most clichéd kind of mugging. But for now, my neighbors remain impossibly civil.

QUESTIONNAIRE
\ After *The Element of Crime* by Lars von Trier \

Isn't this your mother? Isn't this her new husband, the fourth in ten years? Isn't this your sister, the one who survived cancer without health insurance? Isn't this her boyfriend pinned to the ground, arrested again, this time for smoking OxyContin from a sheet of tinfoil behind Pacific Lanes? Aren't you looking out over the Pacific, thinking about all the ways the world has failed you, how your friends got holy on you when you joined the army? All your siblings have different fathers, and you are a father yourself. You have your sons' names tattooed on your forearm in cuneiform script. I know what you're thinking—that's not me, don't be ridiculous, I went to school, I keep current, I value my free time, I have opinions, my passport is stamped. How can you deny your own mother, her cruelties and desperations and beauties floating in you like toy boats? How can you deny your dead grandmother's ashes? How can you deny your new stepfather, who painted the funeral home director's house in exchange for your grandmother's cremation? How can you deny the first minutes after sundown, the fog blowing sideways, and you, and your family, the only family, emptying the ashes into the surf? It's illegal; it's what you're going to do.

STEALING BURROS
\ After *Mon Oncle* by Jacques Tati \

It was only later I learned those burros were stolen. By
way of funeral murmurings. By way of letters, overhead
conversations that, time to time, dropped to the level of
my ears in a room full of voices. Barn light. Dust light.
The voices there. The way you hear about things in a family whose members don't know one another.

John Iron Stride and my uncle stole them from two
brothers in eastern Oregon, somewhere around Hell's
Canyon. Molly and Murphy were mining burros. Dumb
and tough. My uncle and John made saddles and tooled
leather. Why they thought the burros needed stealing no
one knows or cares to tell. The brothers cooked meth and

mined for gold. Everyone and everything in this story is dead now.

My uncle lived in a two-story '40s stick house along the Columbia River. It was built right into the side of the dike. House on one side, Columbia on the other. He owned twenty acres, grew vegetables, and pieced together a living. That summer we drove up as a family to meet other families whose land was to be condemned for the natural gas pipeline. My uncle's property was close to the beginning of the line, ours near the end.

Everyone agreed, the burros were uncommonly beautiful. Even the way they drank water from a clawfoot tub half buried in the mud was significantly breathtaking. We fed them chard from the garden. They'd turn their backs on us every once in a while, stand with their heads touching, and read each other's thoughts.

My uncle asked if we wanted to see something amazing and we said yes. He disappeared into the barn and yelled, "Ready?" From the hayloft above the burros' pen flew three white barred owls, like three ideas for a dream. The last three things you think about before you close your eyes, hoping at least one of them will visit you on the other side.

BLATZ
\ After *Mon Oncle* by Jacques Tati \

Cracked plaster cherubim graced the dirty halls in the tenement building where we lived across from the old tavern that sold Blatz. Sometimes rats swarmed the trash bins in the basement. We kept our plates and mugs and cutlery in plastic bins because of the bugs. No sink in the bathroom, plywood floors we covered with rugs to hide the manufacturer's stamp. The super used to look after us. He had a twin brother who was in a wheelchair, and the first time I saw the brother, I thought the super had been in a horrible accident. Never had any problems except shit in the doorway one time, and a guy got murdered across the street. A large group of young men dressed in red caps showed up to pay their respects to the family. But that was nothing to do with us. I almost forgot about the time some kids on the rooftop down the block shot at me with a BB gun while I was walking home, no way they could hit anything that far away, so I stopped to taunt them. I guess we were like settlers in that neighborhood, but we ourselves looked down on the hipsters who moved into the neighborhood after us. Their appearance presaged a wave of glass condos going up in vacant lots. A car-repair garage became a grocery store selling organic grapes. A place called the Barcade opened up, featuring vintage video games that really attracted the weekend cabs. The Blatz place closed down.

At Christmas when we left town, some kids snuck into our place through the fire escape and took my camera and my old laptop computer and a couple of cheap earrings that belonged to my girlfriend. We had the gall to call the cops, and they made a farce of it, sending two detectives to "dust for prints." The kids in the building didn't talk to us after that, we'd broken the unwritten rules of our arrangement. I stopped greeting them and pretty soon we moved out.

The next guy that moved into the apartment tipped over a candle in his sleep, and the firefighters destroyed two floors of the building with their hoses and axes putting out the fire. The owner would have been thrilled if the whole building burned down: more condos, break the grip of rent control. The super and his brother in the wheelchair and their sons and daughters and nieces and nephews, what about their fates? I wish everybody a boring life in the suburbs with a space-age metal toaster and a two-car garage with an automatic door and a dumb fountain that sprays colored water in garish displays.

THE CANNERY
\ After *On the Waterfront* by Elia Kazan \

I've fallen in love with my own cruelty: I fold the black wings toward the center of its body, and I sew it onto my head like a fashionable hat. I pretend not to notice others pretending not to notice as I stroll along the docks, flipping an imaginary white cane in front of me, tapping the old boards as if punctuating a delightful sentence. When a woman from the cannery walks toward me on her way home from work, she passes right through me. In that moment we are both tourists in my body. Her black rubber boots hum with fish scales that swim in their desire to find the smallest traces of light.

PICTURES
\ After *On the Waterfront* by Elia Kazan \

I should have known you from the very beginning as an informer and a spy. You had the problem of hypocrites everywhere, genuine popularity. You always had friends who hated each other but who both thought *you* were OK, for a while. *You* listened, you understood, you were on their side. When in fact you were on every side. You cheated, then you confessed, and which is more detestable? You became more than one person, and these fictions didn't add up. I hear this tendency starts as a childhood survival instinct, but later on in life, it does no good that nobody knows what you'll do in a situation. The mob sure doesn't like it—they did away with me on your information, congratulations! I'm dead but I'm still around, walking invisible in the fog down where the docks used to be, my shadow crossing the screen of the abandoned picture house where the kissing always got heavy. And when you see me in the mirror, it's something you won't forget.

REASONS FOR STAYING
\ After *Taste of Cherry* by Abbas Kiarostami \

To begin, consider water pouring over the gray marble of the salamander's eye, hard water whose deposits shimmer in goosenecked sink pipes, water that stains the teeth of widows, water and its mineral shadow floating over the city, crossing the new moon, entering the machine of hours.

Or, perhaps, the ocean dressing itself in the echo of its sources. Dead boats, old cable, depth charts, crab pots and their funereal ropes.

The donkeys in the lot at the edge of town, owned by a wild man who shot me more than once with rock salt.

I took girls there, and two-pound bags of carrots, and stroked the animals' long ears in the orchard light.

Finally, the way I hear two, slender, beautifully veined feet stepping out onto the high wire of your voice.

NEIGHBORS
\ After *Taste of Cherry* by Abbas Kiarostami \

I remember the rumors about our duplex, the only rental on the street, how some previous tenants once kept a horse in the garage. The neighbor in the other side of the building carried on with another woman while his wife worked out of town. Things went sour, and he got in his car, started up the engine, and sat in there by himself with the garage door closed, waiting. He hadn't understood that the duplex was so poorly constructed that the fumes would leak through to our side.

He had called his girlfriend before he got behind the wheel. The girlfriend called 911.

I woke up feeling groggy, forgetting where I was, and I knew that something was wrong because I found my mom asleep in her room long after her normal wakeup time. I nudged her awake just as the firemen burst into our house, setting massive fans on the staircases to blow away the fumes. They shouted at us to get out. An ambulance idled outside, but not for us, for the neighbor.

At the emergency room, student nurses stabbed around my mother's arm until they found an artery for a "blood gas" test. Under the hospital lamps she looked like a figure out of Rembrandt.

The funny thing afterward was living next to this guy who had nearly killed us. He didn't seem to be aware that we knew anything about what happened. Certainly he didn't know that the landlord sent us the police report. I'd pass him on the driveway as he went out to get his mail. I was unpleasant to him, never said hello or even smiled. A religious Catholic, he positioned statuettes of Jesus' mother, Our Lady of Sorrows, in the lawn near the walkway leading up to his door. I always wanted to ask him whether he'd try it again, and whether he'd mind bringing us with him to heaven.

UNDERSTUDIES

\ After *Opening Night* by John Cassavetes \

Dressed in their bathrobes, the red tips of their cigarettes slashing through the air around them, Ted and Nancy screamed at each other in the same way, every night, in their front yard, hopelessly drunk, until slowly one neighbor at a time would walk out into the street.

You think you can get to me! You think you know me! You think I don't know what you're doing! You want to hit me, then hit me!

Ted died from asbestosis, Nancy left for California to stay with her sister, and we gather in the private rectangles of light made by our open doorways, facing one another, desperately in need of someone, night after night, to play their part.

CLOSING TIME
\ After *Opening Night* by John Cassavetes \

My mother would wake up late at night and see her dead mother, standing in the doorway to her bedroom, wearing a tattered robe of shadows.

The last time I saw my grandmother before her death she had trouble closing her eyes, which had a dull, filmy sheen about them, like the painted eyes of a shark. When my mom tried to touch her, she turned her face away to the wall. In her younger years my grandmother had been fun-loving—she had been kicked out of a tour at the Vatican for wearing a mini-skirt. After her shock therapy, she drank wine during the day while doing yoga or paced around her house smoking cigarette after cigarette for years on end.

When she died, I drove my mother to the nursing home so that she could sit with the body for awhile. I left the room to give my mom some privacy, but after twenty minutes passed I began to get scared. I went back into the room and told my mother that she had to leave. My mom appeared spellbound, locked into some sort of invisible battle or silent argument with her mother's corpse.

"OK," I said.

"OK," my mom said.

"It's time to go."

"I know."

"So come on."

"All right," she said.

"All right," I said.

When, years later, she came back to haunt my mom, my grandmother stood in the doorway, repeating my mother's name over and over again.

"So it's a dream?" I said.

"Not exactly," my mom said.

"Not exactly?"

"I mean, I know it can't be real, but I do see her."

"It's a dream," I said.

"Do you think I don't know the difference with a dream?" my mom said.

FIGURES IN THE LANDSCAPE
\ After *Carnival of Souls* by Herk Harvey \

There's the abandoned chrome plant off Highway 42. The remains of free-range cattle that hunters found singed into the damp earth. The homemade electronic instruments the conspiracy chasers kept behind their pickup seats. The twenty-three acres my older half-sister and her boyfriend used to own before they lost everything to an investment scam involving the harvesting of brine flies from Utah's Great Salt Lake. The mill workers and professors who shed their worldly husks to follow Bhagwan Shree Rajneesh into the hinterlands of Oregon. The aluminum canister my grandmother used as a table centerpiece that was once part of an incendiary weather balloon the Japanese launched into the jet stream near the end of the war. The 1:16 scale replica of the Kremlin a group of loggers started building but never finished along Wolf Creek. My great aunt Wilma who blacked out the windows in her farmhouse, one window each month, after her husband's death. And there's the myrtlewood box inlaid with turquoise where my father hid a key to the storage unit he rented in secret. Sometimes at night I'd hear the whispers of adults, but maybe it was just the box singing. Eating meatloaf in front of the TV on Fridays, waiting for the right lottery numbers to be drawn. The long weeds and waist-high grass scraping at the house. The nights of my childhood were so dark they looked green, dark as the spinach the gods cooked in pig fat and ate before they drew up their plans to float down to Earth and insert themselves into all our affairs.

DOUBLE DISAPPEARANCE
\ After *Carnival of Souls* by Herk Harvey \

And later, during the mental illness that nearly killed her, my mother told me strange stories. One time, she explained, when her caregiver drove her to therapy, she brought my mom up to the third floor of the building instead of the second floor, where her appointment was supposed to be. There, she saw what she described as an office that looked in every detail identical to her therapist's office, and she met with a woman who looked a lot like her therapist but who was not her therapist. My mom had somehow tricked this other woman who was posing as her therapist, she told me, and managed to escape with her life.

THE MAN WHO MARRIED AN EGG

\ After *Blade Runner* by Ridley Scott \

After my father leaves us, he buys a dozen large eggs and takes a perfectly brown, perfectly egg-shaped egg for a wife. At night he places her in the robin's nest by their wedding photo. By day she sits on the kitchen table in a stand made from a coat hanger. They listen to classical music on the radio and complain about the lack of twentieth-century composers and the DJ's droning, airy voice.

In his letters, he jokes about the dancing lessons she wants but he won't take, weekend trips to national parks, and how they admire the sunset together in their apartment, imagining the gray, rambling city as a vast, red-flecked desert alive with yellow light. His letters are ignored, returned, cruelly answered. Each year he paints another wrinkle on the lovely planet of her face.

WHAT THE BEAST KNEW
\ After *Blade Runner* by Ridley Scott \

So, about this nightmare. My superior officers at the base task me with extracting information from this. . . *creature*. The beast looks like a bunch of loose spinal cords writhing around, with stingers all over. They want me to torture this creature in order to find out a specific piece of information. What everyone needs to know, and what only the creature can tell us, before time runs out, is the answer to this question: "When did you remember you were here?"

DEPARTMENT OF PROPAGANDA
\ After *Gate of Flesh* by Seijun Suzuki \

When I wrote my grandfather's obituary, I included none
of what I'd discovered in the cedar trunk he kept locked
in his gun cabinet. Instead, I redrew my borders and became a vast field of grass swaying in the wind made by
the passing of a massive convoy. Truck after truck passed
by the same green canning jar full of small human teeth.

SEVEN DAYS IN CANNES
\ After *Gate of Flesh* by Seijun Suzuki \

And when he was dying politely in a VA hospital bed, my great uncle Frank asked me to get his photocopied version of his unit's military history in Europe. As I read the narrative aloud, Frank made little corrections and elaborations along the way about dressing up as Santa Claus for crowds of British orphans, slogging through miles of French mud, feeding liberated Russians, guarding bridges against saboteurs, trading occupation postage stamps with Hitler's image blacked out by rectangles of dark ink, looting champagne and cognac from vacant castles. The unit history offered winking thanks to a group of women in Saint-Lô. I noticed that one of these women had the same name as Frank's daughter, my aunt.

"This girl told me she was pregnant just before we left France," Frank said.

"You could have written to her, maybe," I said. "Found her on the Web."

"I never knew if the baby was mine," he said. "I gave her some money."

I asked him what he did when the war ended.

"You mean VD Day?" Frank said, triggering his morphine button. "They gave us a week's R&R. I wanted to go back to Saint-Lô. But they sent me to Cannes instead."

"Seven days in Cannes," I said. "What did you do down there?"

"Anything I wanted."

FOR US
\ After *Antichrist* by Lars von Trier \

I take it you are leaving me because you finally discovered the case of human ears I keep under the bed. I'm sorry if my little collection appalled you. But, to be fair, I did not ask you to open up that little lock with the final unfamiliar key on the ring.

I know you secretly enjoyed the camaraderie of the simulated gas attacks, the socials after the nuclear terrorism drills. But all that was nothing compared with the ears, and I regret that they disturbed you.

You know what I think? I think you're using them, the ears, I mean. As an excuse to leave me. If you really loved me, you might have at least asked how I got them, rather than judging me right off the bat. The answer might surprise you.

It's my job to sell them, door to door. The job was the only way of paying for all those things I bought for the house on the credit card.

The credit card company thugs came in the dead of night. They can do that now. It's you or her, they said. They threatened to *repossess you*. Work with us, they said, and you might be able to keep her.

So now you know where I go every morning. With my suitcase full of ears, up the stairs to the doorbell, excuse me, ma'am, but have you considered the advantages?

I don't mind the ridicule.

But I'm not doing this for myself, Honey Bear. I'm doing it for us.

DIFFERENT FIRES
\ After *Antichrist* by Lars von Trier \

Trish and I started dating during one of those long summers when nearly everyone I knew lost their job, got divorced, and became convinced, through the ramblings of AM radio talk jocks, that the slash piles burning on the logging ridges were actually the ceremonial human sacrifices of Satanic cults.

Trish would only let me undress her if we role-played. It started simply enough—a livestock veterinarian called out to deliver a foal late at night only to find the farmhand's crippled daughter alone in the barn. But then we started doing things like chasing a fistful of diet pills with gin, emptying the knife drawer onto the bed, and going at it until someone cried for mercy.

One time we did it on the ground beyond the guardrail of the ocean overlook, the sun dropping into the horizon like a battle flare disclosing an enemy's location. The orange glow over the Pacific could have been a village on fire—there we were, too far away to send for help, but too close not to admire it.

FALSE FRIENDS
\ After *The Friends of Eddie Coyle* by Peter Yates \

The leaflet at customs informed us that having sex with children was a serious crime. At the bus station, located in a zone of rubble beyond the hive streets of markets and illegal DVD vendors and the crowds of Nicaraguan immigrants lined up outside the consulate, a sign clarified local laws for plying the sex trade. My mistress wanted to see the spider monkeys at the zoo near the peace lodge in the mountains. For transport you could take a taxi for fifty dollars or a bus for five dollars. On the bus you had to watch your things and interact with people who had no financial motivation to pretend to like you. We waited and watched as passengers loaded their possessions in large black garbage bags.

To me the spider monkeys seemed desperately bored, saddened, and attention-seeking, like bad little kids, abused, evil intelligent babies.

"Investigating creatures," my mistress claimed.

They had long spidery legs and arms, plus the tail that, in essence, gave them five limbs to navigate the trees in their spacious pens. One monkey came right up to us at the double chicken-wire fence, stretched himself out on the wire so that if we reached through we could just touch his exposed belly. My mistress scratched him. Afterward the monkey climbed down the wire very slowly and deliberately to the single spot in the enclosure where there was only one layer of chicken wire. There, he fit one whole tiny hand through the little hexagonal openings in the wire. Long, brown, leathery fingers reached out. The hand sort of . . . beckoned. When I told her she'd get bitten, she withdrew. The monkey sulked in a sleeping position, hugging himself and nesting his head like an airline passenger trying to sleep on an overnight flight.

"The human problem is a monkey problem that got out of control," I suggested.

"Thumbs," she said. "Once we got thumbs it was Game Over."

A major earthquake happened a few days after our departure home. A town near the spider monkeys formed the epicenter of the mudslides and damage. That night, my mistress called my wife to cry about it all. There was nothing unusual about that. They worked together.

Of course, I only overheard my wife's half of the conversation. Later, I dreamed my hands became poisonous little spiders.

THE MUSICAL
\ After *The Friends of Eddie Coyle* by Peter Yates \

Among the several ways I died in my sleep this week, the worst was certainly when an old girlfriend took me to see a musical called *Your Inevitable Compliance.*

MY FRIEND WHO CLIMBED
INTO A SENTENCE
\ After *The Bothersome Man* by Jens Lien \

The last place I saw her alive was the bus stop on Al-
berta but it wasn't a bus she ultimately stepped into it was
more like a sentence masquerading as a bus it was winter
as she climbed the steps she turned back to me and said
"It is snowing and it is going to snow" and the O shape
of the last syllable of the last word she spoke entered the
banquet halls of ice and entered into the way the winter
birds nod and greet one another with that same ancient
sound the shape of it the shape she took that O that will
never be filled in to form the only mark that could end
this sentence

STATIONS
\ After *The Bothersome Man* by Jens Lien \

The city seemed so different once you left. I came home
one day from the library and all of our furniture seemed
to be gone. I thought somebody had broken in until I realized that only your possessions were missing. Even the
clear shower curtain with the goldfish printed on it—
you'd just bought it and it still had that new vinyl smell.
I'm pretty sure you weren't just a figment of my imagi-
nation, that we did move in together in the summer, did
make promises in the fall, and then, when the snow began to fall . . . no warning signs. No farewell. No note.
Your phone number out of service, then transferred to a
stranger who asked me to please stop calling, he didn't
know you and he couldn't help. I rode the buses all night,
looping and circling from one end of a line to the other,
putting in eight-hour shifts, exiting at random stations
to see if you might be among the crowds. Eventually
I stayed inside the buses as approaching dawn revealed
stray dogs and abandoned tower blocks on the outskirts.
When I wept openly on the bus, and nobody looked at
me, or during those hours when I was the only person riding, I began to wonder if it wasn't you who had left the
world, but me, if I had gradually begun to turn invisible. Rhythmic patterns of clichéd suicides would form in
my head: *To test if you exist, just stab yourself.* I imagined
that the other passengers could see me only vaguely flick-
ering, like a bad hologram. I couldn't seem to turn up my
voice to make myself audible. I sent away for a medal of

St. Jude from a postal address in Chicago but never heard back. What saved me was a pamphlet that college kids were handing out one day at the station, a map depicting how within fifty years many cities would be inundated by flooding caused by rising sea levels. This cheered me up immensely. I wanted to stay alive to see it happen. I figured we would meet again in a crowded tent city or a trash barge ferrying survivors to wooded areas up along the Great Lakes, where the great future civilizations of Milwaukee, Detroit, and Cleveland would rise.

ANOTHER DREAM
\ After *Dreams* by Akira Kurosawa \

The same changes happened to person after person I knew in college. One day they'd be slumped over a bottle of ether stolen from the chem lab, sleeping with someone else's girlfriend in a carpet of ripped up paper towels, or shouting at everyone from a tree with a wine cooler in hand, and the next thing you know, they'd be taking the MCAT, enrolled in classes at the Learning Annex, studying for the realtor's exam. Life was like a practical joke that never ended in any punch line, or like that magic trick where the colored silk scarves never stopped coming out of your pockets, you have to keep pulling and pulling and pulling long after the audience has gone home

127

and the theater is empty. Based on their vaguely disconnected cheerfulness and lack of intensity, I became convinced that all of my friends were taking the same anti-anxiety medication. The drug had a leveling feature that made everyone unnervingly unworried about everything, except recycling.

"It is what it is," one old friend explained over a low-cal beer. The beer had recently been advertised in a commercial with people getting ready to have sex after working out on exercise bikes in the complimentary gym of their suburban eco-conscious apartment complex. This friend worked on simulations involving loose nukes. When I asked how things were going, he mildly suggested that if I were planning to raise a family that I probably should move at least seventy miles away from any urban center.

I had a bad stretch around age ten when I dreamed nightly of nuclear annihilation after seeing the kill radius depicted on a graphic of the area surrounding my home, but I hadn't thought about those particular nightmares for years.

THE PATTERN
\ After *Dreams* by Akira Kurosawa \

When I close my eyes, I am a scientist. I make a discovery that is too late to matter. What reveals itself from beneath the microscope looks like a date pit—within it I see a beautiful, vast web of numbers. So few people remain that the news of the cure has nowhere to travel. Across the country, freight trains near the detonation sites are fused to their tracks. The trees have lain down within their shadows, and the shadows within themselves. I don't know why, but I've been compulsively working to fill, exactly, one square mile of scorched farmland near the edge of town with box-spring mattresses. I think of the image that will remain after the fabric has rotted from the springs. I will lie down among them. I will enter the house of knowledge. The springs will carry my bones, and I will enter the pattern.

ALL IT TOOK TO GET RID OF YOU
\ After *Solaris* by Andrei Tarkovsky \

I thought I had woken up. Going out into the hall, I noticed that the front door was open. This was unnerving because I was living alone again after the divorce. The last time I had used the door was early the previous evening when I came home from work. Then I heard someone in the house, fussing around in the kitchen.

It was you in your running clothes. You looked hale and flushed, your breath heaving a little, like it did when you first started jogging. I had made fun of you then, thinking it wouldn't last, but it was actually one of those minor changes, like listening to new music or suddenly acquiring a hobby like knitting, that heralds a breakup. What was strange about this situation was that the breakup had already occurred, we had agreed not to call or see each other, the old phrases like "space" and "needs" had been dealt and played, and you had no reason to return to our house. You didn't even have keys anymore.

"Hello," you said, more nonchalantly than was comfortable.

"What on earth are you doing here?" I said.

"How do you mean?" you said, looking hurt in that way that always annoyed me so much. You gestured to the walls around you in the kitchen as if you were indicating ownership, or at least familiarity.

Then I had my big idea:

"You're not you," I said.

"What?" you said, using your *don't be foolish* face that came out during social occasions.

"I just realized," I said. "You're not you."

"I don't understand," you said.

"What I mean," I said, "is maybe you're not who you think you are."

I was trying to give you a hint or clue to the situation we had found ourselves in.

"But I wonder," I added, "if you are also having this same dream right now."

"Oh," you said. "I see what you mean."

THIN AIR

\ After *Solaris* by Andrei Tarkovsky \

My first real girlfriend used to pick me up from my shift at the cannery and drive us to the lighthouse overlook on the Old Coast Highway before she took us back to my apartment. She was convinced she could read my thoughts. I loved riding in her Corvair. Its rear engine and orange factory paint.

I always suspected she was a pathological liar and a hustler.

But there was something so tender about her oddities, the way she moved in with me the same afternoon I met her in the mini-mart at the Cheap-O gas station, the way she had hot-glued green plastic army soldiers across her dashboard, the inside of the windshield, and upside down from the bare metal roof. When reading my thoughts, she would say, "Your mind is like a watercress." The truth is, I liked the way she talked about my past lives, the way we sat with our backs to the dead town I'd grown up in, facing the salty black ink of the Pacific. She entered the rooms of my mind and described in detail how warm or cool they were, how they smelled, how the floors creaked as they settled into the night, how I looked sitting at the desk in the very last and smallest room, how she touched the scar on the back of my head and said she could tell I was thinking about how beautiful she looked. I was happy to give her all I had.

THE OREGON TRAIL
\ After *Stalker* by Andrei Tarkovsky \

During the same week my older brother, Scotty, became
a born-again Christian and started lecturing us at dinner about getting saved and avoiding eternal damna-
tion, my foster brother, Peter, became a devotee of Ancient Astronaut Theory. Moses was a prophet, Moses was
an alien, and the Ark of the Covenant was an ancient alien
weapon—that sort of thing.

For Christmas that year Scotty gave each of us a
wooden cross that he'd carved from cedar and threaded
with long leather string. They were too big to be neck-
laces, but we all wore them that day, on the outside of our
clothes—even Peter. Scotty opened our traditional Christ-

mas dinner at the Spaghetti House with a retelling of the trials of Mary and Joseph, then led us in a prayer that required us to hold hands.

In secret, Peter gave me a mail-order pewter button of a Mayan figure with a serpent's head, whose shape resembled a delta-wing jet and proved the existence of advanced ancient technology. "A guy in Baltimore built one of these, but fifty times bigger, and it flew perfectly," he had said.

Scotty threatened to disown my parents and punched Peter, hard, in the face, one night when we were all playing along with *Jeopardy*. Blood got everywhere. During a commercial break, Peter had shown me a book he checked out from the public library arguing that Sacagawea, Joan of Arc, and Jesus were benevolent, shape-shifting extraterrestrials determined to save us all from ourselves. That winter, Scotty's girlfriend's father—a county commissioner—fired my father from his janitorial job at the county courthouse.

Each spring, for the next twenty years, my father will use a toothbrush and a bucket of bleach to scour all the moss and black mold from the stone figures in the statue garden at city hall. Lewis and Clark, frozen in place, one holding a map and squinting into the horizon, the other looking through a spyglass at the fire in the sky.

PENS
\ After *Stalker* by Andrei Tarkovsky \

It could happen: a drinking glass slides across a table by itself when no one else is watching. The first assumption would be mind control, but maybe ordinary objects themselves contain magic, or else they're haunted. I've seen the same thing happen with this box of pens, typical red office pens I found in my grandfather's desk after his death. Sometimes the box contains six pens, sometimes seven—one of the pens inhabits a parallel universe. For some reason, nobody can own this particular pen. I tried lending it out to several friends but it always returns to its box within a day or two. Another of the pens writes in invisible ink, only revealing its script when tea is spilled on the paper. One pen writes only lies, still another leaks blood, and yet another somehow bends my hand to compose sentimental letters asking for acceptance and forgiveness from old lovers and lost friends. (The ink for this pen appears inexhaustible.) There's a pen I'm afraid to use or even talk about after what I saw it produce. And then this one last pen, perfectly normal, another bit of mass-produced plastic, tinted like an artificially colored cherry, with the letters "MAPC" stamped on the side, just like all the rest. It's the pen I love the most, even though it doesn't do anything extraordinary.

RÉSUMÉ
\ After *Mirror* by Andrei Tarkovsky \

Forgive this slight digression. In the Soviet Union, in the year I was born, 7,500 meters of film translated into one feature-length movie if you used three takes or fewer per scene, on about 600,000 rubles, resulting in seventy-three copies of a picture that screened almost nowhere in Moscow. The filmmaker had to steal from everyone—his father's poems, his actors' souls, pictures from Brueghel, the coffers of the state, even a poster of one of his own early films. He planned to use a hidden camera on his own mother, and then to put this footage of her into his film. Nearly forty years later, the film has outlived its filmmaker and outlasted the nation that paid for it to be made.

Do you see my point? I am trying to explain why I am uniquely qualified for this position. Yet another empire is crumbling outside this cinema. Onscreen and off, China's being blamed in some way, for everything, again. Do you get what I'm driving at? It's unsettling to discover images from your own dreams in someone else's movie. Does your health benefits package include inpatient coverage for mental problems? I'm only asking out of mild curiosity; this is strictly hypothetical. I'd like to apologize in advance if I sound overly negative, this won't affect my performance on the job in any fashion you'll be able to discern immediately.

Personally, I've never been all that fond of mirrors—the metaphors associated with them are clichés, and actually I find it unnerving to watch myself aging so blatantly year after year. But this movie contains the history of everything and, I like to think, the seeds of an apology for all imperial thinking, if I might put it that way. Goskino—the official state production company that funded this picture—might have rejected it outright. But somehow it snuck through. It snuck through! My God, think of that!

My wife believes that the female lead in the movie eerily resembles one of my ex-wives, but they are utterly unlike in every way imaginable except for their love of proofreading. After we watch the movie, we talk: what are the things that matter? Acceptance of failure, plus noticing and listening to people and things. I still don't understand anything, obviously. I know I'm not supposed

to ask, but will I get this job? What is it that you're looking for. . . ?

THE GOD OF CHILDHOOD
\ After *Mirror* by Andrei Tarkovsky \

More than my mother waiting in the car while my young-
est brother and I crept through the aisles of Safeway to
steal a roll of orange "Dollar Off" stickers from the Meat
Department. And more than the dense black spark puls-
ing at the center of my parents' refusal to go on food
stamps. More than the speech therapy I received from
our family friend who ran a dog-grooming business from
her kitchen and moonlighted as a faith healer. More than
the laying on of hands. More than the broken ribs of the
moon falling through the trees. More than every tree falling through every night in every wind storm. More than
the silent, white fields that I knew existed in other parts
of the state, where time ran at the same speed as the gathering snow. The rain. It could fall for years at a time. But
more than the rain. More than mudslides and sinkholes.
More than the union picketers at the shipyard and more
than the scabs. More than amphetamines and drag racing
at the old airstrip. And more than bonfires. And more than
my best friend whose father burned down their house for
the insurance money, with the entire family inside, and
more than how he staged their rescue and became, for a

time, a hero of our town and the cause for bake sales. And more than fire itself. More than huffing gas-soaked washcloths from plastic bags behind the Gas-N-Go. More than everything was how I decided, from an early age, that the parallel universe could be entered at will. But "parallel" doesn't get it right—more that I could see the inner lives of everything. My father, dragging a piano without casters by a fraying rope through the graveyard shift, my sister slicing through the night on a glittering trapeze. My brothers bound to one another by baling wire as they stumbled toward their mediocrity. My mother juggling handkerchiefs beneath a cone of light, faint blue smoke hovering around her. And me, in every mirror I looked into, every school-bus window, in every black cup of coffee, I could see the God of Childhood, which, from the moment it landed on my head with its light, hollow bones, to that stretch of years where it rode in my shirt pocket each day, its animal heart beating wildly against my chest, to the moment I released it when I turned forty, it pulled me through everything by its rein of starlight. Even with all that passed now, I still carry one of its feathers pressed between the pages of this book, the spine creaking like a great barn door opening out into the dusty sunlight and the rolling fields of all my future days, the long grass bent to the east, asking the wind for forgiveness.

COMMUNIQUÉ

\ After *The Sacrifice* by Andrei Tarkovsky \

We have been told it is worse in every direction, that it is safest to stay exactly where we are. We have been told it is best to divorce ourselves from the old system and adopt the new system. Handbills fall from the sky with instructions to seal off the windows and doors. The dishes shake in the cupboards. The hills are mute as fish and appear to glow. I can hear vines grow up through the lake and reach for the moon like the hair of the dead.

GODZILLA
\ After *The Sacrifice* by Andrei Tarkovsky \

The summer before the attacks, I took my son to visit the World Trade Center. They had a system where they would take your photo at the lobby, in front of a cardboard back-drop of the Twin Towers, before you went up to the ob-servation deck. You could buy the photo for twenty dol-lars when you were high on the view. They didn't glass you in, and I noticed that my son was inclining his head slightly upwards and had his arms spread out like a paper airplane. Birds passed below us, clouds, city, islands, then the sea. My kid started flapping his hands up and down very quickly, and I remembered how I used to do the same thing when I was a child, in dreams where I hovered over houses and lawns. On our next trip to the city we avoided the site, but my son wanted to see the scale model of New York City out in Queens. It was an exhibit in which every building had been meticulously reconstructed in an enor-mous room. The Twin Towers were still standing, nobody could bear to knock them down, but they had a pink rib-bon wrapping the two skyscrapers together.

My son stamped around on the walkway above the model city, miming the crushing and kicking over of buildings with his feet, then opening his mouth and roar-ing silently like a prehistoric beast.

"I'm Godzilla!" he said.

"Spare Queens," I said.

I should probably tell you that my son is invisible. Other people can't see him standing there by my side in the tourist photo from the Twin Towers, and nobody but me heard him speak in the exhibition, where we stood above the helpless cardboard city. I wouldn't say that he's an imaginary boy, but it is true that he doesn't seem to age. He tells me it's better to imagine that the world is filled with invisible children.

THE FILMS

Antichrist by Lars von Trier, 2009

An Autumn Afternoon by Yasujirō Ozu, 1962

Blade Runner by Ridley Scott, 1982

Border Radio by Allison Anders, Dean Lent, and
    Kurt Voss, 1987

The Bothersome Man by Jens Lien, 2006

Burden of Dreams by Les Blank, 1982

Carnival of Souls by Herk Harvey, 1962

Coup de Torchon by Bertrand Tavernier, 1981

Cría Cuervos by Carlos Saura, 1976

Devilfish by Jean Painlevé, 1928

Donnie Darko by Richard Kelly, 2001

Dreams by Akira Kurosawa, 1990

The Element of Crime by Lars von Trier, 1984

For All Mankind by Al Reinert, 1989

The Friends of Eddie Coyle by Peter Yates, 1973

Gate of Flesh by Seijun Suzuki, 1964

George Washington by David Gordon Green, 2000

Harlan County USA by Barbara Kopple, 1976

Intergalactic by Nathanial Hörnblowér, 1998

Jesus' Son by Alison Maclean, 1999

Life During Wartime by Todd Solondz, 2009

Manufactured Landscapes by Jennifer Baichwal, 2006

Miami Vice by Michael Mann, 2006

Mirror by Andrei Tarkovsky, 1975

Mon Oncle by Jacques Tati, 1958

Mon Oncle Antoine by Claude Jutra, 1971

Morvern Callar by Lynne Ramsay, 2002

On the Waterfront by Elia Kazan, 1954

Opening Night by John Cassavetes, 1977

Overlord by Stuart Cooper, 1975

Puce Moment by Kenneth Anger, 1949

Ratcatcher by Lynne Ramsay, 1999

The Sacrifice by Andrei Tarkovsky, 1986

Salesman by Albert Maysles, David Maysles, and
    Charlotte Zwerin, 1968

Solaris by Andrei Tarkovsky, 1972

Something's Got to Give by Ari Marcopoulos and
    The Beastie Boys, 1992

Stalker by Andrei Tarkovsky, 1979

Taste of Cherry by Abbas Kiarostami, 1997

Vagabond by Agnès Varda, 1985

ACKNOWLEDGMENTS

The authors would like to thank the editors of the following journals, where some of these stories originally appeared: *Bat City Review*, *Blackbird*, *Hubbub*, *Mid-American Review*, *The Rumpus*, and *Tin House*.

Special thanks to the Lannan Foundation, the Creative Writing Program at Stanford University, and the VCUarts Cinema Program for support during the writing of this book.

Deepest gratitude to our editors and publishers at A Strange Object, Jill Meyers and Callie Collins. Additional thanks to Margot Volem, Emily Mitchell, Amanda Coplin, Monica King, and Tina Gerhardt.

Information on the films and other key facts were derived with gratitude from Wikipedia, IMDb, and criterion.com. Details on the production of Tarkovsky's *Mirror* were derived from *Time within Time: The Diaries, 1970–1986*, by Andrei Tarkovsky, translated by Kitty Hunter-Blair (Faber, 1994).

ABOUT THE AUTHORS

MICHAEL MCGRIFF'S books include *Home Burial,* a *New York Times Book Review* Editors' Choice selection; *Dismantling the Hills*; a translation of Tomas Tranströmer's *The Sorrow Gondola*; and an edition of David Wevill's essential writing, *To Build My Shadow a Fire.* He is a former Stegner Fellow and Jones Lecturer at Stanford University, and his work has been recognized with a Lannan Literary Fellowship and a grant from the National Endowment for the Arts.

J. M. TYREE was a Truman Capote–Wallace Stegner Fellow and Jones Lecturer in Fiction at Stanford. His writing on cinema has appeared in the BFI Film Classics series of books from the British Film Institute, as well as in *The Believer, Sight & Sound, Film Quarterly,* and in the anthology *Created in Darkness by Troubled Americans: Best of McSweeney's Humor Category* (Knopf/Vintage). He works as an associate editor of *New England Review.*

ABOUT A STRANGE OBJECT

Founded in 2012, A Strange Object is a women-run, fiction-focused press in Austin, Texas. The press champions debuts, daring writing, and good design across all platforms. Its titles are distributed by Small Press Distribution.